Also available by Tanya Michaels

Falling for the Sheriff
Falling for the Rancher
The Christmas Triplets
The Cowboy Upstairs
Claimed by a Cowboy
Tamed by a Texan
Rescued by a Ranger
Her Secret, His Baby
Second Chance Christmas
Her Cowboy Hero

THE COWBOY'S TEXAS TWINS

TANYA MICHAELS

MILLS & BOON

First Published in Great Britain 2018
by Mills & Boon, an imprint of HarperCollins*Publishers*
1 London Bridge Street, London, SE1 9GF

ISBN: 978-0-263-26474-6

38-0218

FSC
www.fsc.org
MIX
Paper from
responsible sources
FSC™ C007454

This book is produced from independently certified FSC™ paper to ensure responsible forest management.

For more information visit: www.harpercollins.co.uk/green

Printed and bound in Spain
by CPI, Barcelona

Thank you,
Johanna Raisanen and Kathleen Scheibling,
for years of encouragement
and brilliant editorial suggestions.

Chapter One

When Grayson Cox left town at eighteen, he'd sworn hell would freeze over before he ever moved back. Now, ten years later, his stomach clenched as the truck's headlights hit the Welcome to Cupid's Bow sign. *Hope the Devil likes ice skating.*

Grayson still couldn't believe he was taking Aunt Vi up on her offer, but he had a damn good reason. His gaze darted to the rearview mirror, and he checked on the passengers behind him. *Make that* two *good reasons.* His godsons, twin five-year-olds, were asleep in their booster seats, each leaning toward the other, so close their blond heads were almost touching. The two and a half weeks since their parents' funeral had been full of upheaval—tears, bad dreams, acting out; this rare moment of peace reminded Grayson of the morning they'd been christened, cherubic infants who hadn't even cried when the priest poured the water.

Blaine had heckled him before the ceremony for getting the twins confused in their matching christening gowns. "What kind of loser can't tell his own godsons apart?"

Grayson had responded with the same mock-derision. "What kind of loser picks a bull-riding rodeo bum as a godfather? Don't you know any respectable people?"

At that, Blaine had squeezed his arm. "A few, but they ain't family."

Neither were Blaine and Grayson—not technically. But they'd been as close as brothers, and Grayson had doted on Miranda, his honorary sister-in-law.

I can't believe they're gone. He swallowed hard, fingers clenched around the steering wheel. Grayson was no stranger to tragedy—he'd been orphaned at fifteen—but even he had trouble processing a twist of fate this cruel. His own father wrapping a car around a tree in a drunken stupor had probably been inevitable. But Blaine and Miranda Stowe had been big-hearted, wonderful people enjoying their first romantic vacation since the boys were born when their charter plane crashed in Mexico. As a guardian, Grayson would never be able to fill their shoes, but he would try his hardest to do right by the twins.

Which meant finding a better place to live than the one-bedroom trailer he'd used as a home base between rodeo competitions and seasonal ranch jobs. He also needed to find a stable income—and someone to help watch the boys while he was earning said income. Aunt Vi to the rescue. Again.

As he crossed the cattle guard that was a holdover from years past, when his late grandfather kept a few cows on the small farm, déjà vu gripped him. He remembered pulling in to this same yard with Aunt Vi after his father's funeral, her assurances that he'd get used to his new home. *She was younger than I am now.* There were only nine years between him and his mother's younger sister. Violet Duncan must have been terrified at the prospect of taking in an angry teenager, but she'd never shown it. Until he'd met Blaine at a rodeo outside of Waco, Vi had been the only person in his life he'd ever been able to count on.

And how did I thank her?

He tamped down the rush of guilt. He had other things to worry about now besides not coming home for holidays or a truckload of teenage misdeeds he hoped she'd never learned about.

There was a carport to the side of the white one-story house, but the space next to Vi's car was taken up by a large doghouse. So Grayson parked on the grass. He barely had the key out of the ignition before porch lights came on and the front door swung open. Violet hurried out of the house with a mismatched pack at her heels—three dogs of varying size and color. When he'd lived here, it had been cats—a calico named Xena and a deaf white cat named Baby Blue. Aunt Vi took in strays of all species. When she'd come to cheer him on at a rodeo championship a few years ago, she'd told him about a seventeen-year-old girl who'd stayed for a month while her parents screamed through the worst of their divorce.

Grayson couldn't predict what the boys would think of Cupid's Bow or the kindergarten class they'd be attending once he got them enrolled, but they were sure to love the big-hearted redhead who baked some of the best desserts in the state.

He swung open his truck door and hopped down to hug her. "Sorry it's so late." He'd decided that the drive would be easier after dinner, when the boys were likely to fall asleep instead of getting bored, fretting about the relocation or bickering with each other. "You didn't have to wait up for us."

"Pffft. I'm a night owl anyway. You know that." She kept her voice low as she glanced over his shoulder at the sleeping twins in the cab.

He chuckled. "If the three barking dogs aren't waking them up, I don't think you have to whisper."

Ignoring his teasing, she reached for the truck door. "I'll get the little guy on this side, if you want to go around to the other."

"I can carry both of them." Honestly, he'd lifted saddles that were heavier than the twins put together.

She balled her fists on her hips. "I'm not even forty, Gray. Hardly frail."

"No, ma'am. I just meant, they're so scrawny." Some of that was inherited body type—Blaine was tough but wiry, Miranda was slim—but Grayson worried. "I think Sam's losing weight. I can barely get him to eat."

The light spilling from the truck was enough for him to see the sympathy in Vi's expression. "Just give him time. And maybe some of my peach cream-cheese pie. It was your favorite, remember?"

"I remember." In the months before his father's fatal car accident, Violet had frequently dropped by the house with baked goods. As an adolescent with a bottomless appetite, Grayson had thought she was just being nice. Looking back, he suspected the visits were her way of checking up on him—and on Bryant Cox's drinking.

In a way, Grayson's father had abandoned him just as his mother had years earlier. Except, Rachel Cox had left in one fell swoop, disappearing entirely from Grayson's life and never looking back. Bryant had deserted him drop by drop, glass by glass. *Lord, let me do better by these boys than my parents did by me.*

Luckily, it wasn't a very high bar to clear.

Once the twins were unbuckled, he and Vi each took one, falling in step as they approached the house.

"The four of us should go to the grocery store tomorrow afternoon," she proposed. "Let the boys show us their favorite foods, and I can plan some cooking projects. Kids are more likely to eat something they feel invested in."

"Sounds good." Even better, it sounded *simple.* The last few weeks had been so overwhelming. Deciding which belongings to bring with the boys and which to leave in storage. Gathering all the records needed to transfer them to Cupid's Bow Elementary. Creating a to-do list of new parenting tasks. He needed to memorize their allergies, find a pediatrician, consider whether they would benefit from grief therapy. In comparison, picking up dinner ingredients at the supermarket was so easy, he felt light-headed with relief.

Vi had left the front door standing open when she came out to greet him. The smallest of her canine pack dashed past Grayson on the porch stairs, nearly tripping him. As he steadied himself, Vi made an apologetic noise behind him.

"Sorry, should have warned you. I give the dogs treats when we're all in for the night, and Shep gets a little greedy for hers."

"No harm done. I've got to start doing better about watching where I walk anyway. I stepped barefoot on one of the boys' Legos last week and thought I was going to cry. Those suckers hurt."

Inside the house, she told him, "I'm putting the boys in your old room and you can sleep on the twin bed in my office. Is that okay for tonight? We can figure out different arrangements if—"

"Vi, *you're* doing *us* the favor," he reminded her. "You could put me in the doghouse and I wouldn't complain." Considering a few of the cheaper motels during his early days on the rodeo circuit, the doghouse would not be the worst accommodations he'd ever experienced.

The bed in Grayson's former room was a queen-size, with plenty of space for two little boys to share it without bumping into each other or accidentally pushing each other off the mattress. But the second Sam and Tyler were tucked under the sheets, they rolled toward each other, as if seeking comfort.

Gray reached for the lamp on the nightstand. "I'll get some night-lights, but can we leave this on for now? Tyler's a tough little dude during the day, but he hates the dark. The last thing I'd want is for him to wake up scared in an unfamiliar place." He shoved a hand through his hair. "Maybe I should have timed the drive differently, so that we arrived during the day and they'd have a few hours to acclimate."

"Don't second-guess yourself. If they'd spent the afternoon in the new place, they might have been too anxious or excited to fall asleep. You'll be right next door if they need you tonight. In the meantime, they look like they're getting much-needed rest. What about you? When was the last time you got eight hours?"

His laugh was hollow. Over the past decade, he'd trained himself to sleep anywhere, from noisy hotels with thin walls to the ground on occasional cattle drives. But the last decent night's sleep he'd had was before the phone call about Blaine and Miranda.

"I keep a bottle of emergency whiskey over the fridge," she said. "Think a slug of that would help you sleep?"

"I don't touch alcohol."

"Understandable. Hot tea, then? I'm going to have some lemon balm. Valerian is relaxing, too."

He wrinkled his nose. "Thanks, but I'm not really a hot-tea kind of guy. All I need is a glass of water and...maybe a cookie?"

"I baked a fresh batch of oatmeal cranberry last night."

They made their way to the kitchen, where the smallest dog—a mixed breed with the coloring of an Australian shepherd but the implausibly short legs of a dachshund or corgi—was impatiently turning circles by the counter, whimpering for her nightly treat.

"That's Shep," Vi said. "The one-eyed beauty behind you is Tiff and the golden doodle who grew a lot bigger than his former owner's expectations is Buster."

"You and your strays." Thank God she was so willing to open her doors to anything that needed refuge. *I hope the boys like animals.* "You must have the biggest heart in Texas."

She looked away, her expression troubled. "Oh, I don't know. I've had my share of selfish moments, made my share of mistakes. In fact..."

He reached for the Holstein-patterned cookie jar, so delighted to be back in this kitchen that it took him a moment to realize she trailed off. He might hate the surrounding town—the place where everyone knew his mom hadn't wanted him, where classmates bullied him until his freshman growth spurt, where his dad's drinking was public knowledge—but all of that mattered a little less at Violet's kitchen table. "You were saying?" he asked as he pulled out three cookies.

"Never mind. You've already had a long day. Plenty of time for us to talk later." She stuck her head in the pantry and emerged with a box of tea bags. "It's so weird. Sometimes when I look in your direction, I still expect to see a dark-haired kid with two front teeth missing, not a six-foot cowboy."

"Whereas *you* never age," he said fondly. "If hot tea is your secret, maybe I should rethink turning it down."

"Pffft. The laugh lines are increasing, the red in the hair is fading and working at home has destroyed any sense of fashion I may have once possessed." She held her arms wide, showing off the ancient University of Texas shirt she wore with purple plaid pajama shorts.

"You're gorgeous. You look like that actress..." He snapped his fingers. "Jessica Chastain."

"Uh-huh. Spoken like a guy sucking up to get baked goods."

Grinning, he bit a cookie in half. "Mmm. It's been too long since I had these."

"Maybe you should have visited more."

Shame flooded him. He'd sent her tickets to watch him in the rodeo and had even convinced her to spend a sandy Christmas at a beach resort with him, but he knew his unwillingness to come to Cupid's Bow had stung her. She'd deserved better. At eighteen, he'd been so hell-bent on leaving that he'd gone the day after his last high-school exam, depriving her of even watching him walk across the stage a week later to get his diploma. "Vi, I—"

"Don't worry about it. I was teasing, and I shouldn't have. You have a lot on your plate right now and don't need me guilt-tripping you. Sorry."

"*I'm* sorry. You must feel taken for granted, with me staying away until I needed a huge favor."

"The favor was my idea," she reminded him. "And I'm happy to help. That's what families do."

Theoretically. His mother had apparently missed that memo. *At least I have an aunt who loves me.* Blaine, who'd grown up in the foster-care system, had been less lucky.

"I am beyond grateful. And I promise, I won't take advantage of the situation, leaving all the parenting to you. These boys are my responsibility. I won't be a slacker guardian, but day cares are expensive, and it could be up to a month before the life-insurance money comes." More than a babysitter, though, what he really needed was a second opinion. Last summer, Blaine had accepted a promotion that moved his family to Oklahoma so it had been nearly a year since the boys had seen Grayson. He must seem like a stranger to them, and he had no idea what he was doing.

Self-doubt scraped him raw. "Every decision I make feels like a trap. Honest to God, Vi, I've had broken ribs that hurt less than the worry I'll somehow make this worse for them."

"I felt the same way. I think everyone questions their ability to raise kids—biological parents, adoptive parents, experienced parents who already know the ropes. But you can do this. Imagine it like bronc riding. It won't be easy, but you hold on and hope for the best."

And pray you survive.

Chapter Two

"It's always the quiet ones."

Hadley Lanier glanced up from the computer, where she'd been entering a request for a book transfer from one of the county's sister libraries. "Hey, Becca." She grinned at the strawberry blonde. "Or should I say Madame Mayor?" Even with all the months that had passed since her friend had been sworn in, Hadley was still thrilled. Becca was terrific for Cupid's Bow, a natural leader. And, on a more selfish note, Hadley had helped with the campaign, so she considered herself a tiny part of the victory. "What quiet ones are you talking about?"

"You." Becca set a stack of books on the library counter, the top one a thriller with blood-red letters across the cover. "Of the nine women in our book club, *you're* the Quiet One, but—"

"I am?" Hadley was shy as a kid but hadn't thought of herself that way in years. Straight A's in school had bolstered her confidence, but the real breakthrough had been on the softball field, with a crowd cheering her on from the bleachers. A pang of nostalgia went through her, and she absently rubbed her shoulder.

Becca frowned. "Well, yeah. But maybe that's just in comparison to the rest of us because we're such loudmouths. You know how Sierra is, and I've been bossy since birth. So you come across as the sweet, quiet one. But I just finished the book you picked for tomorrow, and, quiet or not, you have a dark side."

"You didn't like it?"

"It was well-written—very well-written—but a little disturbing. I may have to check beneath the bed before I can sleep tonight."

"I would have thought a big strong cowboy like Sawyer in the house makes you feel extra safe," Hadley teased.

Becca's mouth curved in a soft smile at the mention of her fiancé. "There are definitely perks to having him around. But when book club rotates back to you to pick our selection, maybe something without a serial killer next time?"

"Deal." Hadley liked to alternate between her two favorite genres, anyway—creepy suspense novels that made her heart race and romances that made her heart race for different reasons. Bookworm cardio.

They chatted for a few more minutes about what snacks they were each bringing to book club tomorrow and about their friend Sierra, who was getting married in June. Both Becca and Hadley were in the bridal party. Then Becca's little boy, Marc, approached the counter with his selections from the children's library.

After Hadley checked out their books and waved

goodbye, she glanced at the clock. Closing time. On Sunday, the Cupid's Bow Public Library was only open from one to five. This was her shortest workday of the week, and it had gone by fast. There'd been a steady flow of students needing resources for projects due after spring break and citizens wanting to use the free internet. She gently reminded the two people still on computers that it was time to go, then went through her end-of-the-day ritual of shutting everything down and making sure the restrooms were empty.

She grabbed her purse and headed for the double glass doors at the library's main entrance, faltering at the flock of large black crows that dotted the lawn. They were all facing the library, as if they'd been waiting for her.

This is why you shouldn't read scary books, dummy. They only spur your overactive imagination.

Real life frequently made her think of some story she'd read. When she'd been eight and walked out of a store to encounter two ladies dressed in antique gowns and bustles, she'd believed for a full second that she'd time-traveled. But, no, the women had been handing out flyers for a historic reenactment. *Well, you're not eight, anymore*, she reminded herself as she rubbed away the goose bumps on her arm. *You're a mature, rational twenty-seven.*

In her defense, the sky was overcast, uncharacteristically dark for this time of day, which could give anyone a sense of foreboding. Deciding that a friendly voice would be a good distraction, she pulled out her cell phone as she crossed the deserted lot.

Her older sister, Leanne, answered on the first ring. "I was just thinking about you!"

"Something good?"

Leanne snorted. "I was mentally cussing you out for talking me in to night classes. Why did I think I could go back to school after all these years? I'm not as smart as you."

"You're plenty smart! You were just…easily distracted in high school."

"Boy-crazy, you mean."

Not everyone would catch the edge of regret in her offhand tone, but Hadley knew her sister well, knew there were decisions she wished she could take back. "I only pushed you to go back because I know you can do it."

"I hope you're right. Studying for this bio exam is kicking my butt."

"Why don't you come over for dinner in about an hour?" Climbing into her car, Hadley reached for the seat belt with her free hand. "I'm leaving work now. I'll stop at the store, grab something easy to cook and help you study."

"That sounds great—as long as we can eat something besides barbecue." Five nights a week, Leanne waitressed at the most popular barbecue place in the county. The Smoky Pig regularly graced tourism lists of top Texas barbecue restaurants, and it stayed busy.

"Hmm…now that you mention it," Hadley joked, "barbecue sounds pretty tasty."

"I'm hanging up on you, brat."

"See you in an hour."

It only took Hadley ten minutes to reach the grocery store, but by the time she parked, the heavy clouds were accompanied by a brisk wind and rumbles of thunder. No lightning yet, but there was an almost tangible electric charge to the air. It rushed over her skin, making the hairs on the back of her neck stand up.

She doubled her pace, hoping to get in and out of the supermarket before the storm broke. Grabbing a cart, she formulated a mental shopping list. Pasta with shrimp was quick and simple, and she could round out the meal with a salad. As she made her way toward the seafood counter at the back of the store, a crash reverberated. Not thunder this time, but something closer and more difficult to identify. Had it come from the next aisle?

She heard the scolding murmur of a man's deep voice, followed by a high-pitched wail. Then a little boy yelled, "You made my brother cry!"

"Sam, I didn't—Tyler, don't..." The man's voice was slightly panicky as he tried to shush the unhappy children. "Boys, please!"

His ragged tone made Hadley want to help. Besides, she didn't recognize the man's voice, and she was unabashedly curious. Her mother used to say it was a toss-up as to what would get Hadley into more trouble—her overactive imagination or her need to investigate situations that were none of her business. Momentarily abandoning her cart, she peeked around the corner at the cereal aisle.

Boxes were everywhere. Among the cardboard wreckage, one boy sobbed facedown on the floor while another sat a few feet away, making similar noises. Yet his eyes were suspiciously dry, as if he wasn't so much crying as expressing solidarity. It took her a second to realize the boys were identical. Meanwhile, a broad-shouldered, dark-haired man was trying to placate them while simultaneously righting the freestanding display that had been toppled.

She cleared her throat softly. "Need a hand?"

The man whipped his head toward her, almost guiltily, and she got her first clear look at him. Hair so dark it was almost black was brushed upward from his forehead. The short style emphasized the masculine beauty of his square, stubbled face; granite was softer than that jawline. "Sorry about the disturbance, ma'am."

Flashing him a reassuring smile, she kneeled to retrieve a dented box of cornflakes. "This hardly qualifies as a disturbance. You should see the library on story day when half the preschool audience needs a nap."

He gave her an answering grin, and dimples appeared. Oh, mercy! His muscular body had been impressive even before he turned around, but now that he was smiling and his eyes shone with—

"What the heck happened here?"

Hadley glanced past Dimples to find a bewildered Violet Duncan, holding a bag from the pharmacy while she gaped at the sobbing boys and scattered boxes. Violet was a web designer who volunteered her skills to keep the library's online community calendar updated.

The horizontal twin lifted his tearstained face and responded, "It w-w-was a accident!"

"Grayson yelled at Sam!" the other twin accused.

Grayson…

Good Lord. Dimples was Grayson Cox? Hadley hadn't recognized her former classmate. She knew he was Violet's nephew, of course, but she'd been under the impression that his visits to Cupid's Bow were as rare as unicorns. Was he in town for their high school's ten-year reunion next Saturday? And who were these little boys? With their brown eyes, she might have guessed they were his except the kid had called him Grayson, not Dad.

"I did not yell!" Grayson defended himself. "I told him to stop running, which he didn't, and then I pointed out the consequences of not listening." He gestured at the mess around them.

Violet scooped up Sam and set him in the shopping cart. The action startled the boy out of his crying.

"I'm too big to ride in the cart," he protested.

"You're also too big to throw temper tantrums in the grocery store," Violet said mildly. "If I let you walk, will you quiet down?"

With one last dramatic sniffle, Sam nodded.

"Good. If you and your brother will behave, you can come help me pick out something for dessert tonight." With a sigh, she turned to Grayson. "You want to finish restoring order here and meet us in the baking aisle?"

"Yes, ma'am." He ducked his gaze, looking as boyishly chagrined as young Sam.

When Hadley chuckled at his expression, all eyes turned to her.

Violet gave her a wan smile, acknowledging her as she shepherded the boys away. "Hey, Hadley."

"Hadley?" Grayson echoed, turning back toward her. He blinked. "Hadley the Cannon?"

"No." The quick denial felt like a protective gesture, warding off the once beloved nickname. "I mean, no one calls me that." Not since she was seventeen.

"But you *are* Hadley Lanier?" He studied her from top to bottom, the intensity in his gaze making her shiver. Like her, Grayson had brown eyes, but his were a few shades lighter, nearly the color of her dad's favorite bourbon, ringed in a circle of darker brown that made his eyes unforgettable.

She couldn't believe she hadn't recognized him sooner—or that she had yet to look away. *Quit staring.* Easier said than done.

Outside, she'd felt the prickle of storm-charged electricity against her skin, but that was nothing compared to the sizzle that went through her now. "I, uh… What was the question? Oh!" Her cheeks burned. "Yes. I'm Hadley."

His hand clenched around a cereal box as he scowled at her. "What the hell are you doing here?"

Chapter Three

Grayson hadn't meant to blurt out the question so rudely. But the idea of Hadley Lanier in Cupid's Bow was almost as ridiculous as his being here.

Her eyes narrowed, their coldness making him belatedly realize how much he'd been enjoying her earlier warm interest. "I'm grocery shopping, same as you. But without toppling displays and making small children cry."

Less than twenty-four hours in town, and they'd already made a public scene. Yeah, he was really winning at this parenting business. "I didn't mean what are you doing here in the store," he said impatiently. "Why are you in Cupid's Bow? Last I saw you, you were headed off to play college softball, with big plans to get your diploma and see the worl—"

"Plans change."

Ain't that the truth. He felt a spark of kinship with her, probably his first ever. During their school years, he'd spent a lot of time annoyed with her. Even before high school and her blind devotion to Reggie George, Grayson had hated the excited class reports she gave about other countries. Her vivid social-studies presentations about all the places she planned to see made him realize how big the world was, how many places his mom could be. While he was cooped up in a classroom, listening to some stupid report from a know-it-all girl, was his mother swimming in an ocean? Surveying Paris from the top of the Eiffel Tower? Whether she'd been in Paris, France, or Paris, Texas, the result was the same—his own mom hadn't loved him and all his classmates knew it.

"Hello, Hadley, dear." At the other end of the aisle, a stooped elderly woman nudged her cart forward and stopped in front of the hot cereal. She eyed Grayson with open curiosity. "Would one of you be so kind as to reach the grits for me?"

"I'd be happy to, Miss Alma." Hadley smiled, but the expression seemed forced—especially when she cut her eyes toward Grayson. "We were done here anyway."

No, they weren't. Curiosity about her life choices aside, he needed a chance to apologize for his rude bluntness. *You're a role model now, remember?* He could just imagine Aunt Vi's response if she heard how he'd spoken to Hadley. Probably something like "You want people to think I didn't raise you with any manners?"

Stalling, he fussed with the cereal display, making sure the boxes were perfectly lined up while he waited until he could talk to Hadley alone again. He listened with half an ear to Alma's chatter. "How's your mama, dear?" and "Looks like some storm blowing in" and "Who's the hottie?"

"Miss Alma!" Hadley sounded mortified, and Grayson registered *he* was the "hottie" in question.

Grinning inwardly, he darted a glance toward his former classmate. With her hair pulled back in a long, loose ponytail, he had a clear view of her face turning pink. He remembered that about her from high school, that she'd been prone to blushing. Her jackass boyfriend would pass her notes, their contents guessable by the color of Hadley's cheeks. Oh, hell, what if the jackass boyfriend was why Hadley had settled in Cupid's Bow? He could be the jackass husband by now.

When Hadley caught him looking at her, she planted her hands on her hips. "I suppose you're referring to Grayson Cox, Violet's nephew?" Hadley asked Alma. "I don't see anything 'hot' about him."

Alma snorted. "Then you should make an appointment with Dr. Shaffer to get your vision check— Oh! Violet's nephew, you say?" She lowered her voice to a whisper.

Grayson's stomach churned. He hated knowing he was the topic of discussion. Gossip had followed him throughout childhood—people talking about his mom's disappearance, his father's drinking, his aunt taking him in when she was so young. There were townsfolk who thought Violet and Jim McKay had been on the verge of getting engaged before Grayson disrupted her life; he'd always been too afraid to ask her if he was the reason she and Jim had ended things.

There was a break in the whispering, and Hadley

cast him a quick look over her shoulder. Instead of her earlier irritation, now there was pity in her eyes. Screw it. He didn't need to apologize *that* badly. Time to get out of here. He strode away from the reorganized cereal display, but Hadley caught up with him, nearly matching his stride. She was a tall woman. Though she'd been known on the softball field for her pitching, she could haul ass around the bases when necessary.

He kept his eyes straight ahead. "I take it you got an earful?" How much did Cupid's Bow citizens already know about his moving back?

"Apparently, Alma heard from Dagmar, the florist, who overheard Violet tell the sheriff's wife that you and your godsons… Grayson, I'm sorry about your friends."

His breath caught, a painful knot in his lungs. He couldn't talk about them. Logically, he knew Blaine and Miranda were never coming back—he'd had to remind the boys of that on several heart-wrenching occasions—but he still hated discussing it. As if talking about their death made them *more* dead somehow. He gurgled an inarticulate response to her condolences.

"I can't imagine how difficult this is for you. Which is saying something," she added, wry humor edging into her sympathy. "Because I have a very vivid imagination."

He was surprised she'd made a joke about herself instead of dwelling on his situation. Some of the pressure in his chest eased, and he offered her a tentative smile.

"That's why I didn't recognize you," she murmured.

"Excuse me?"

"When I first saw you in the cereal aisle, I didn't know it was you."

Ditto. Grayson hadn't reconciled the curvy stranger with the girl he'd known. In his memory, she was either in a softball uniform or snuggled up to Reggie George.

"You smiled when I offered to help," she explained, "and those dimples are an effective disguise. The Grayson Cox I went to school with never smiled at me."

"Don't take it personally." He hadn't done much smiling at anyone during his adolescent years.

She hesitated, then shook her head. "I better run. I have company coming for dinner, and I'm behind schedule."

"Hot date?" he asked before he could stop himself. He didn't see a wedding band or engagement ring, but she could still be dating Reggie. Then again, Hadley was smart. Despite her long-ago loyalty to her boyfriend, surely she'd figured out sometime during the last decade what an entitled bully he was.

"My sister, actually. And if I don't get my butt in gear, she'll reach my house before I do." She turned back to her abandoned cart.

"Hadley? I'm sorry I was so abrupt earlier. The boys and I just got here last night, and I'm…adjusting. To, um, everything." Cupid's Bow always brought out the worst in him.

"Maybe you can make it up to me with a cup of

coffee sometime," she said lightly. "It would be nice to catch up with an old friend."

"We were never friends." How could they have been, when he'd spent so much time holding everyone at arm's length? Never mind that she'd been dating his nemesis.

"No, I guess we weren't." Her dark eyes flashed with hurt.

Crap. He hadn't meant to insult her. "But like you said earlier…things change, right?"

She nodded, not looking entirely convinced. "I guess we'll see."

"OW, DAMMIT!" HADLEY yanked her hand back from the pot. As she'd dropped pasta into the boiling water, her thumb had grazed the metal.

Leanne paused in the act of uncorking the wine. "You need me to finish up cooking? You've been distracted since I got here. You're lucky you didn't catch your sleeve on fire lighting the burner."

"I've got it under control now." Possibly. "Besides, you shouldn't have to help cook. You're the guest."

"Big sisters don't count as guests. What's on your mind, anyway? Thinking about one of your stories?"

"No." Until Hadley had sold a couple of short stories to a mystery magazine last year, it had been a well-kept secret that the town librarian also dreamed of being an author. She was still hesitant about discussing it, but her sister had been super supportive. Leanne was the one who'd recently encouraged her to apply for a unique writer-in-residence opportunity. "I was thinking about new friends. Or old friends, I guess. If it was an old friend who wasn't actually your friend."

"Uh..." Leanne held up the chardonnay. "Did you finish one of these without me before I got here?"

"Ha—I barely had time to carry in the groceries, much less down a bottle of wine. I had a strange encounter at the supermarket." She lowered her voice the way she used to when making up ghost stories to thrill her sister when they were kids. "On this stormy night, I ran in to a tall, dark man from my past."

"For real? Last time I went to the grocery store, the most noteworthy thing that happened was I had to wait ten minutes for a price check."

"Grayson Cox is back in town." At Leanne's blank look, she added, "He's my age and was kind of a loner. You might not remember him."

During Hadley's junior year in high school, her older sister had run off with a man nearly a decade older. She'd declared him the love of her life, but it only lasted four months. By then, she'd had a waitressing job in Albuquerque and soon landed in an even worse relationship. Although she sounded miserable whenever Hadley talked to her on the phone, she'd been too proud to come home. It wasn't until after their mother's stroke that Leanne returned.

"Grayson is Violet Duncan's nephew," Hadley elaborated. "Bryant Cox's son?"

"*Oh.* His dad was the one who crashed into that big oak tree on Spiegel."

Fatal car accidents were rare in Cupid's Bow; that one had made a lasting impression on everyone. As

Hadley recalled, Grayson hated being defined by his dad's death. She'd witnessed him get into more than one fight in the high-school cafeteria.

"So you and Grayson were friends?"

"Um, no. Not in the strictest sense. We didn't hang out with the same crowd." Hadley had always been with her softball teammates and their collective boyfriends, and Grayson had been…apart, scowling from the outskirts. Once, she'd tried to apologize to him for her boyfriend's obnoxious idea of a joke, but Grayson had made it clear he wanted nothing to do with her. Or with any of them. "He could be abrasive, guarded. But people change, right?"

Leanne, reconciled with her once estranged family and working toward a college degree, should understand that better than anyone. "Is that why he's back in Cupid's Bow? Because he's a changed man?"

"Personal emergency brought him back." She took the glass of wine her sister offered. It seemed wrong to gossip about Grayson's circumstances, especially given how uncomfortable he'd looked in the store, but with the way information spread, Leanne would hear all about him in the Smoky Pig anyway. "I don't know the specifics, but he's here for his aunt's help. He's raising two little boys after a friend died."

"That's terrible." Leanne sipped her wine in silence. As Hadley was plating their food, she asked, "So was your encounter with him actually out of the usual, or were you just being dramatic?"

"I, uh…" Her reaction to him definitely hadn't been typical. When he'd flashed those dimples at her, heat had coursed through her. She'd been so captivated by his smile that for a second, she'd forgotten about the surrounding mess or the noise of crying children. And when he'd rejected her offer of coffee, her disappointment had been irrationally powerful, too. She wanted to see him again. She wanted—

"You're *blushing*! Let me guess, former grump Grayson Cox grew up to be good-looking."

Extremely good-looking. "Are you implying I'm shallow?"

"I'm saying you already know most of the men in a fifty-mile radius, and none of them has put that look on your face lately. You should ask him to be your date for the reunion."

"Oh, good grief. I just told you, he's dealing with a lot right now. He has real priorities, and I doubt dancing in the Cupid's Bow High gymnasium with some girl he barely remembers makes the list." She carried the plates to the table. "Now, sit down and eat. No one should have to study on an empty stomach."

After dinner, they spent an hour and a half on biology. "You're so much smarter than you give yourself credit for," Hadley said as Leanne was packing up her notes. "You need to have more faith in yourself."

"Uh-huh. And what were your exact words when I suggested we should go suitcase shopping because you'll need luggage after you win that writing residency in Colorado?"

Hadley's face heated. Every time she thought about the application she'd sent in, she felt equal parts excited and nauseated. "I love that you believe in me, but I'm a longshot at best. Some of the applicants have probably published actual books, and I… Okay, I see your point. I guess we could both work on our confidence."

Her sister nodded. "And you know what's a good exercise for boosting self-confidence? When you ask a hot guy to your high-school reunion and he says yes."

"Leanne! We covered this already. Now, if we're done with the academics, I have some writing to do tonight."

"You're just saying that to get rid of me."

"No, I'm saying it because it's true. Getting rid of you is a bonus."

"All right, I'm leaving. But when you become a rich and famous novelist, you have to take us on a fabulous spa weekend."

"Deal."

After locking the front door behind her sister and changing into a pair of yoga pants and her favorite Snoopy T-shirt, Hadley curled up on the couch with her laptop. As much as she loved her job at the library, this was her favorite time of day—when she got to play with words like they were clay, molding her own world and shaping fascinating characters.

Except, tonight, the characters weren't cooperating. The lanky inspector from Scotland Yard suddenly bore a striking resemblance to a rugged cowboy, and none of his dialogue came out right. After typing and deleting half a dozen attempts at the same sentence, she relented. For the moment, perhaps her time would be better spent on story research than the actual writing. She opened the search engine, preparing to fact-check the form of poison her villain used. But her fingers didn't cooperate any better than her characters had. Instead of typing *arsenic trioxide*, she inexplicably typed *Grayson Cox.*

I am going to do story research. Really. Just as soon as she finished skimming a few articles about a certain rodeo champ.

GRAYSON WIPED A damp hand across his already damp jeans, noting that there seemed to be more water on *him* than on either of the two boys in the tub. But, silver lining, Sam and Tyler were both clean; Grayson had helped them wash their hair without anyone yelping about shampoo in his eyes and everyone seemed recovered from the earlier incident at the grocery store. He still wasn't sure how they'd gone so quickly from a simple "Boys, no running" to total meltdown.

Yet, without the resulting meltdown, Hadley never would have poked her head around the corner to help.

Despite past irritations with her and the graceless way he'd handled their conversation, he didn't regret seeing her. For one thing, she was a lot of fun to look at, with her dark shining eyes and full lips. He recalled her suggestion that they meet for coffee sometime. If he was successful in finding a job, who knew how long he and the boys would be in Cupid's Bow? It would be nice to have a friend. Then again, a curvy brunette friend who'd stared at him with alternating interest and disappointment might be a complication he didn't have room for right now.

He turned his attention back to the twins, who were

happily splashing around like a couple of river otters. "All right, you two, if we don't get you out, you'll wrinkle into prunes." He held up a towel. "Who's first?"

They'd progressed to the pajama stage—Grayson helped Tyler correct course before he inadvertently stuck his head through the sleeve a third time—when Vi rapped her knuckles against the partially open door.

"Need any help?" she asked.

"I think we're good now." Except for the state of her bathroom. "But if you want to read them their story, I can mop up—"

"You won't be there for story?" Sam's eyes grew huge.

Grayson rocked back on his heels, meeting the boy's gaze. "I was just going to let Violet read tonight so I can clean up the mess we made."

The boy thrust his bottom lip out. "You hafta stay with us! 'til we fall asleep."

Tyler nodded solemnly.

Grayson ran a hand over his jaw. His guess was that if you let kids dictate your actions, you ended up with spoiled monsters. But the twins were coping with extenuating circumstances. He stood. "Tell you what, I'll straighten up in here while you two take this stuff to the laundry room. Violet can show you where, if you forgot." He balled up their dirty clothes and a towel from the floor. "I'll meet you in your room in time for story, okay?"

This met with everyone's approval, but even forty minutes later, as Sam yawned and his eyes fluttered closed, a note of apprehension lingered in his voice. "You'll be here tomorrow?"

"Absolutely," Grayson said. "I'll be here every day." The enormity of his responsibility hit him anew. He was looking at years, decades, of trying to figure out what was right for these kids.

"And Violet will be here, too? And Tiff and Buster and Shep?"

Buster lifted his head from where he was lying at the foot of the bed, thumping his tail in reassurance. The boys had befriended the dogs immediately.

He squeezed Sam close. "We'll all be here, buddy." Grayson did have one appointment tomorrow—for a job interview Vi had arranged—but he'd remind the boys about that in the morning. For now, he just wanted Sam to feel secure. He understood the question the boy was really asking: are we going to get left again by the people we love? *I miss them, too, buddy.*

Once Sam finally yielded to sleep and both boys were softly snoring, Grayson padded down the hallway to the kitchen. Where the cookie jar lived.

He drew up short at the sight of his aunt working at the kitchen table. Her laptop and a mug of tea sat in front of her. Client folders were scattered across the surface. *Because she gave her office to me.* "I've displaced you."

She glanced up with an absent frown "What are you talking about?"

"The boys and I will find a house when I have the money for it," he vowed. "We won't inconvenience you forever."

"I get to work in my jammies with a dog lying across my feet. My life couldn't be any more convenient. Boys asleep?"

He nodded. "When I was trying to decide which of their belongings were critical to keep with us and which could be left in Oklahoma for now, I overlooked the importance of bedtime stories. I've read the same four books so often I've memorized them."

"Take the boys to the library. All the bedtime stories you could want." Her lips twitched in a small smile. "Just ask Hadley."

He choked on a bite of cookie. "H-Hadley?" His mind got hung up on the brunette mentioned in the same sentence as bedtime, and the tips of his ears burned the way they had when Vi had caught him kissing Julia Yanic on the living room couch thirteen years ago.

"Yeah, you should ask Hadley for children's book recommendations. She is the town librarian after all."

Oh. Right. Hadn't she mentioned something about story hour at the library? "Weird. Not the part about her being a librarian. She always loved books." He had a sudden stray memory of her carrying around a large book of wonders of the world in middle school, asking him if he wanted to know how many kilometers long the Great Wall of China was. "But I can't believe she's stuck in Cupid's Bow."

Violet sighed. "I realize your childhood wasn't idyllic, but some of us like it here."

Some people, maybe, but not his mother. Her own son hadn't been enough to hold Rachel Cox here. "I didn't mean to sound so derisive. I just thought Hadley was going out of state for college, headed for bigger things."

Vi's brow furrowed. "I don't remember all the details, but there was something about her getting hurt and losing her softball scholarship to college."

"Damn," he said softly. "Does life work out for anyone?"

"Plenty of people. *I* can't complain."

Couldn't she? She'd spent her twenties raising him and now here she was in her late thirties taking on his problems again.

She scowled, her tone firm. "Quit being so negative. Is that how you want the boys to view life? Hopeless?"

"No, ma'am."

"Good. Then start looking for the hope around you. And if you don't see any, do the world—and yourself—a favor. Create some."

Chapter Four

Grayson kept half his attention on the twins playing air hockey at the child-sized table behind him, and the other half on the apologetic blonde behind the front desk. He knew it had been a long shot to ask if they were hiring here. The community center was staffed largely by volunteers and high-school seniors, who coached little kids' basketball. But he'd decided that since he was dropping off Vi anyway, it couldn't hurt to ask.

"We're just not hiring right now for any of our full-time positions," the blonde said. "If there's a specific area of expertise you think the community will find useful, you can sign up to teach one of our six-week classes. We've done whittling, self-defense, introduction to Spanish… Otherwise, all I can do is take your name and number and let you know if anything opens up." She passed him a clipboard and a pen. "Oh, and if you could list two local references, that would be useful."

He grimaced, having gotten a similar request at his interview this morning. The construction foreman said he typically preferred three references; he was willing to bend that rule as a favor to Vi. He might also be swayed by Grayson's roofing experience after high school and willingness to do manual labor in the Texas heat. But if the construction job didn't work out, Grayson would need local references for his next interview. It suddenly struck him how many times he'd written Blaine Stowe's name on forms; his best friend and honorary big brother had been everything from a character reference to an emergency contact.

After filling out his contact info, Grayson thanked the woman for her time and handed back the board. Then he collected the boys and they departed. The plan was to run to the nearby library while Violet had her meeting.

"We'll check out some books and then, if there's enough time before Vi's ready to go, you two can play more air hockey. Or we can walk through the rest of the center and see what other activities they have," he said as he started the truck. "And just wait until summer comes! Cupid's Bow has a really huge pool. You'll love it." He'd promised Vi, for the boys' sake, that he'd focus on the positive.

His aunt was certainly an inspiration for positive thinking—and for positive action. Her meeting today was with Mayor Johnston and a few other citizens to discuss starting a peer mentorship program where, instead of turning to adults, teens having a difficult time could help each other.

This morning, as they'd cleaned up the breakfast dishes, Violet had said she believed teenagers were more likely to be honest about their problems with kids their own age. Plus, she believed that some teens branded as troublemakers would be motivated to turn themselves around when given responsibility as a peer counselor. That part of the conversation had him choking on his own guilt. Should he confess to his aunt the teenage crimes he'd gotten away with or leave the past alone? She'd worked so hard to shape him into a good person. It would devastate her to learn what a mess he'd been. At the time, he'd convinced himself he was in the right. His rebellions had felt like justice.

After Grayson's mom left, his father had blamed the town, saying Rachel had hated it here, that Cupid's Bow hadn't been good enough for her. Looking back, Grayson could see through his father's excuses, his inability to accept that perhaps he'd failed somewhere as a husband. But as a child, Grayson had bought in to his dad's finger-pointing. At least when he listened to his father's bitter diatribes, Bryant was paying attention to him. So Grayson had been a rapt audience as his dad ranted about everything from the town ruining his marriage to the former business partners who'd screwed him over.

By the time of his father's crash, Grayson harbored a simmering resentment toward most of the people around him, made worse by the pitying gossip about the "orphaned Cox boy." He'd sought anonymous revenge in stereotypical misdemeanors, from graffiti and shoplifting to stealing a high-school mascot. He'd smashed the mailbox of the loan officer who'd rejected his dad's application, a financial setback that resulted in the eventual loss of the store where Bryant met Grayson's mom. Grayson had reasoned that if his dad still had the store, he wouldn't have doubled down on his drinking. If Bryant Cox got that loan, he would have still been alive.

That's not how alcoholism works. Grayson knew that now. But, as a grief-stricken high-school freshman, he'd followed his dad's example—making excuses, lashing out, blaming others. As amazing as Violet had been, no one person could single-handedly undo the emotional damage that came from years of secondhand rage. Only with time, perspective and friends like Blaine had Grayson regained his balance.

He wasn't proud of his teenage self, but he didn't have to be that person anymore. *I'm mature now. And well-adjusted.* More or less.

To prove it, he climbed out of the truck with a friendly smile on his face, reminding the boys about using their "library voices" as they unbuckled their booster seats.

Just inside the front door of the library, a glass display case caught the twins' attention. It was full of trains—or, at least, artistic representations of trains. There were paintings and drawings of varying quality, clay sculptures and a colorful model assembled from cardboard. Above the display was a sign announcing that next month's theme was horses, inviting all the kids of Cupid's Bow to participate.

He remembered the homemade Christmas cards Miranda used to send him and a framed sketch she'd done of the boys sleeping when they were just babies. "You guys like art projects?"

Tyler nodded enthusiastically. "I like to finger-paint. It's messy. Red is my favorite color."

"One time, Mama helped us do an art with sand," Sam added. "It was real messy."

"And we played with shaving cream on our art table. It's squishy. And—"

"Let me guess," Grayson said. "Messy?"

The boys chorused "yes" amid chuckles. He wasn't convinced they'd inherited their mother's artistic sensibility, but they were decidedly pro-mess. He made a mental note to get tarps before attempting any big projects at Aunt Vi's.

They walked into the library, cool from the humming air conditioner and quiet after the sounds of Main Street. A sense of calm washed over him—until he turned and found himself eye-to-eye with Hadley Lanier.

"Grayson!" She appeared startled, clutching a stack of books against her to keep from dropping them. But then she smiled, her dark eyes as sweet as hot chocolate. "Nice to see you."

It was a warmer welcome than he deserved, and he grinned back at her. "You, too. Can I, uh, help you with those?" Did he sound like an awkward seventh grader, offering to carry a pretty girl's books to her locker?

"Sure. I was going to display these on top of the shelves for National Poetry Month." Passing all but a few of the books over to him, she smiled down at the boys. “Hello, again. I’m Miss Hadley. What kinds of books do you two like to read?”

“Do you have anything with dinosaurs?” Tyler asked. Sam didn’t answer, too busy studying his surroundings.

“We have an entire shelf on dinosaurs. That’s our children’s section.” She pointed to a smaller room, walled in glass and decorated with lots of bright colors. “If you two want to go in there and start looking around, I’ll help you find some dinosaur books in just a moment. Does that sound okay?”

Pausing only long enough to give her a brief nod, Tyler scampered off. Sam hesitated, looking nervously at Grayson.

“I’m going to help Miss Hadley move some books,” Grayson said. “You can stay with me if you want. Or, if you want to go with your brother, you’ll be able to keep an eye on me through the glass. Your choice, buddy.”

The boy swallowed. “You won’t go far?”

“Promise.”

Reassured, Sam turned and followed after his twin. Grayson felt a tug of pride. The tiny display of independence might not seem like much to someone who didn’t know Sam, but the boy had been understandably clingy in the past few weeks and this was progress.

“You’re good with him,” Hadley said. When he turned to her meet her gaze, her smile became mischievous. “Much better than I would have guessed after the cereal-aisle debacle.”

“Not one of my finer moments. But I hope I’m getting better. They deserve that. This has been so hard for them—their parents, the move. Starting school in the next week or so. I hope they have an easier time at Cupid's Bow Elementary than—" Was he really about to whine to a beautiful woman about his childhood? Lame. "So, where did you need these books?"

She raised an eyebrow at his abrupt change of subject but didn't call him on it. "Right over here."

The shelves in the library weren't all the same height. Units taller than Hadley lined the walls, but the center was dominated by shorter bookshelves topped with various objects—spotlight collections, winning science-fair projects from the local schools and potted flowers that brought a touch of spring inside.

She led him to a shelf with available space on top, and took a moment to position the books she held before turning to him for a few more.

He passed over the first few without paying much attention, but then a red book cover made him do a double take. "Erotic poems?"

Hadley's head jerked up. "Shh. This is a library, remember."

"Sorry. I was caught off guard."

"By a book? In a library? Yes, what are the odds?" She laughed.

She had a great laugh, he noticed. It trilled out like music, her own personal jingle or theme song.

"These are poems from the 1930s, a part of our literary history, pieces that found beauty and sensuality to celebrate despite difficult times. It's not like they're internet porn."

"So, you've read them?"

"I've read almost everything in the library," she said matter-of-factly. "Most of these books were here long before I became head librarian."

"Now you can read about the Great Wall of China whenever you want."

She cocked her head, her expression puzzled. "Sure, I guess. My first choice is usually historical suspense. Or romances. And don't you dare laugh at that," she said preemptively, as if others had judged her preferences. "I know some people think happy endings are silly, but—"

"Not silly." His heart twisted as he thought of how much Blaine and Miranda had meant to each other, their dream of growing old together. "Just improbable."

There was a clattering sound in the background followed by accusatory shouts of "I didn't do it. *You* did." And "Not my fault!"

Crap. Grayson pressed a palm to his forehead. It was the cereal aisle all over again. Apparently, gravity was no friend of five-year-olds. "I'd better go clean up whatever they just destroyed. Please don't ban us from the library," he implored over his shoulder.

The boys met him in the doorway, their eyes wide. "It was a accident," Sam said. "I just wanted to see the octopus."

A large orange stuffed animal was on the ground, its eight legs in the air as if reaching for help. It was surrounded by children's books that had no doubt been on display until Sam had reached for the octopus and knocked everything down.

"Thanks for the help," Hadley said cheerfully. "The

children's room was next on my list. I was going to swap out the marine-life books for books about sports. Of course, I normally put books carefully back on the shelf instead of dumping them on the floor, but to be fair, your way was quicker."

Sam and Tyler exchanged shocked glances.

"So we're not in trouble?" Tyler asked.

"Accidents happen." Hadley kneeled down to grab the octopus. "Just try to be careful with the books you take home. And never, ever mark in them with crayons or pens, okay?" After extracting that solemn promise, she rose. "All right…dinosaur time!"

She took each twin by the hand, and a few minutes later, each of the boys held a nonfiction picture book about dinosaurs.

"Oh, and this one," Hadley said. "It's about a dinosaur who has to learn to be more careful because he's *so big* he knocks things over and steps on them without meaning to. Like a couple of junior T. rexes I know."

Tyler laughed outright, then made a *rawr* noise at her; even Sam smiled shyly.

They all headed back to the circulation desk so Grayson could sign up for a library card, and the boys asked if they could look at the trains again while they were waiting. Since it was within his sight line, Grayson agreed. "Put your hands in your pockets, though," he suggested. "So that you don't accidentally leave any fingerprints on the glass." Or shatter it somehow.

Hadley handed him his new card and the books. "They're due in a week, but you can renew online if you want to keep them longer. Anything else I can do for you?"

"Actually, yes. But it's a personal favor."

She arched an eyebrow. "How personal are we talking?"

"Well, not like erotic-poem personal—"

"Grayson!"

"Shh." He grinned, charmed by the pink that washed over her cheeks. "We're in a library."

Despite her glare, she was obviously fighting a smile.

"I've started interviewing for jobs," he said, "and I've already been asked for local references. I don't suppose..." It was difficult to voice the request, hypocritical to ask her to vouch for him considering how short-tempered he'd been with her in the past. Why had he been such a jerk? It hadn't been Hadley's fault that reports of faraway places set his teeth on edge. And it hadn't been her fault that her steady boyfriend was an SOB—although Grayson had been disappointed someone with her smarts couldn't see through the guy.

Maybe Grayson had been jealous of her standing in the community. Since the day his mom left him behind, he hadn't felt as if he belonged in Cupid's Bow, and with each passing year, he became more of an outsider. Hadley Lanier had been beloved by teachers and friends and teammates; she was probably adored as town librarian. People like her made it look so easy to fit in, but he knew what it was like to feel other people's whispers like fire ants on his skin.

"Grayson? You okay?"

How long had he been standing here, scowling silently? "I don't know what I am." Dammit, he was supposed to be showing her his good qualities so she could rave about him to potential employers. He shook his head. "Being back here has fried my brain. I swear Cupid's Bow brings out the worst in me."

"That's a shame, since it sounds like you'll be here awhile." She pursed her lips. "Were you about to ask for my phone number?"

"What? No, I—"

"To put down as a reference?"

"Oh. Yes. That is, if you're willing."

She held out her hand. "Got a phone on you?" When he passed it over to her, she typed in her contact information. "There. Now you have my number for job references and picture-book recommendations. Or to, um, invite me to lunch sometime. Maybe all you need to get along with Cupid's Bow better is the right tour guide."

Was she kidding? "I grew up here—not much you could show me I haven't already seen."

"Do you ever read mystery novels?"

"One or two."

"They're all pretty similar. Someone gets killed, someone figures out *who dunit.* It's not like the format is a surprise. But they're all different, too, because they're told from different points of view. The reader gets to see the plot unfold through a new character's eyes. Maybe you just need to see Cupid's Bow from another perspective."

He wasn't convinced, but, for now, Cupid's Bow was the boys' home. He owed it to them to try. "What about tomorrow? Are you free for lunch then?" The question was surprisingly liberating. So much of his time since becoming the boys' guardian had been spent planning, worrying, regrouping. It was a relief to do something as simple as ask an attractive woman to share a meal with him. "Or do you work all day?"

She stared for a second, as if expecting him to retract the invitation. "I, ah... Bunny Neill, the semi-retired librarian who ran the place before me, makes sure I get lunch hours and every other Wednesday off. I'd love to—"

"Is it time to go yet?" Sam loudly demanded from the front entrance.

Grayson winced. "I'll talk to him again about his library voice, I promise."

"I'll let it slide," Hadley said with a grin. "But just this once."

THE WALK FROM the truck to the community center got a lot longer when the boys got distracted watching roly-poly bugs on the sidewalk. Grayson didn't mind. It was a sunny spring day, and Vi hadn't texted yet that she was ready for her ride home, so he slowed his walk to a relaxed amble, letting the boys take their time.

When an older woman carrying a yoga mat exited the building, he scooted the boys to the side to let her pass. The woman nodded to Grayson with a smile, but then stopped short.

"Grayson Cox?"

"Um, yes, ma'am." He tried to place her but it took him a moment to match the friendly woman in relaxed athletic wear with the history teacher who'd worn buttoned-up blouses and disapproving scowls. "Ms. Templeton?"

"That *is* you." Her smile spread. "What a delight to have you back in town!"

It was? She must recall his eighth-grade history class differently than he did.

"Will you be staying long?"

"I think so." He nodded toward Sam and Tyler. "I have an appointment to sign them up for school tomorrow."

"Wonderful. If they're half as bright as you are, they'll—"

His bark of laughter was involuntary. "I don't mean to interrupt, but are you sure you don't have me confused with another student? You gave me a lot of Cs." And more than a few lectures.

She glanced down her nose at him in a gesture he recognized. "Why do you think I was so hard on you? Because I knew perfectly well how bright you are and wasn't about to reward you for coasting by on minimum effort. But you certainly grew out of that! My nephew and I were at the rodeo last summer and happened to see you ride. I can't begin to imagine the bone-jarring effort that takes."

"Th-thank you." If anyone had asked him when he was thirteen, he would have sworn Ms. Templeton hated him. His phone began ringing in his pocket, signaling that Vi was finished.

"I'll let you get that," Ms. Templeton said. She gave him one last smile. "Welcome back home."

He stared after her, almost too bemused to answer Vi's call. "Hey," he said once he'd regathered his wits. "All done?"

"Yes." Vi's voice was tight. She didn't sound as if the meeting had gone well.

"Okay, the boys and I are right outside the front doors."

She hung up and a moment later, he saw her striding through the lobby. Before she reached the exit, however, two men in tank tops and shorts crossed her path. Grayson squinted, realizing that the one carrying a basketball was Jim McKay, Violet's ex-boyfriend. Were they on friendly terms? For Vi's sake, he hoped so. In a town this size, you were bound to run in to an ex from time to time.

With the men standing in front of her, he couldn't see Vi's expression, but when she came through the door a few minutes later, her movements were stiff and jerky, her smile of greeting brittle.

"How was the library?" she asked, her voice slightly higher than normal as she projected gaiety.

"We got dinosaur books!" Tyler said.

"And saw Miss Hadley," Sam added.

"Great. Maybe you can read to me back at the house," Vi said.

When the boys turned toward the truck, Grayson asked in a low voice, "Everything okay?"

"Not really. It might be a two-fingers-of-whiskey-and-bubble-bath kind of night." She shook her head. "Forget I said that. I'm supposed to be setting an example for you in positivity, not bitching about town politics."

"You've always been an excellent example," he assured her. "But I'm a grown-up now. Feel free to vent if necessary."

It wasn't until the boys were asleep after dinner that Vi finally took him up on his offer.

He returned to the kitchen, where she was loading the dishwasher. "I can do that. In fact, I insist. It's the only division of labor that makes sense. If *I* cook and *you* clean, we'll all starve."

She chuckled, no doubt reminded of her attempts to teach him how to cook; he had not been a star pupil. "Thanks."

"If you're not in a rush to get to that bubble bath, I'm a pretty good listener."

"I appreciate it, but there's nothing much to tell." She slid into a chair at the table. "I was just annoyed when I left my meeting. This town is full of wonderful people—but Sissy Woytek isn't one of them. She's opposed to my mentorship idea, kept interrupting me to point out that parents want to keep their kids *away* from troublemakers, not pair them up as buddies. She was so freaking condescending about it." She cocked her head, pursing her lips and imitating a snooty accent. "'If you'd ever married and had children yourself, Violet, you'd understand.'"

"She did not say that!" The seventeen-year-old rebellious punk inside Grayson wanted to find Sissy's address and toilet-paper her house. But then Grayson remembered he was supposed to be building a life for the boys here, not antagonizing pillars of the community.

"Don't worry, the mayor shut her down. And who cares what Sissy thinks of my personal life, right? But running in to Jim McKay on top of it didn't help my mood."

Grayson's memories of his aunt's ex-boyfriend were indistinct. When Grayson had moved in with Vi, he'd been too preoccupied with anger and grief to bond with the man. A few months after Violet got custody of Grayson, the boyfriend had disappeared. She hadn't wanted to discuss it then. Did she now?

"In a town this size," he said tentatively, "you must see him a lot."

"Occasionally. This is only the second time since his divorce, though. And it's the first time he wanted to stop and chat." She pinched the bridge of her nose. "He wants to hire me to create a website. I told him I'd evaluate my current workload and be in touch tomorrow."

He closed the dishwasher. If her current work schedule was so unmanageable that she was turning down paying jobs, he needed to be careful that he and the boys weren't eating up too much of her time. "If the twins or I are interfering with—"

"Gray." Her laugh was part amusement, part exasperation. "Don't you recognize a flimsy excuse when you hear one? I told Jim that because I wanted to sleep on it before I make a decision. I was worried it might be awkward to work with an ex. What do you think?"

It was difficult to relate because there was no one

in his dating past he would have strong feelings about seeing again, no one he'd connected with that deeply. Miranda had once accused him of being afraid of relationships, but his short-lived romances were a function of his being on the road so much. Most women liked boyfriends who were available on special occasions and weekends.

But this was about Vi. "How much would you really need to work with him?" he asked. "Don't your customers email you information and images for updates? It seems like the personal contact would be minimal."

"It depends on the client. I always try to start with a face-to-face meeting, though, to make sure we're on the same page. I need a sense of the image they want to project and I like to make sure they have realistic expectations about what I can do for them."

"Would it be difficult to sit through a meeting with him? Do you...still care about him?"

"What? No! I mean, sure. I care about everyone in town—even Sissy Woytek. But Jim and I are ancient history. *Pre*historic, even. The man was married for six years." She went to the pantry. "I wonder if I have the ingredients to make brownies. Want some brownies?"

He'd seen Violet cope with so much—her big sister's disappearance, her father's death, her sudden custody of a teenager. He knew how strong she could be, how calm in a crisis. It was surreal to see her flustered. Whatever her feelings for Jim McKay, the man had made an impact.

"Vi, can I ask you a personal question? When I moved in, and you and Jim ended things..." *Was it my fault?* He'd taken up a lot of her time and he knew he'd curtailed any overnight stays; she wouldn't have wanted to set that example for him. But the question caught in his throat. It was hard to ask when he feared the answer—assuming she would even tell him the truth. It would be in Violet's nature to protect him with a reassuring lie. He cleared his throat. "I just never understood what happened."

She turned to put an arm full of baking supplies on the counter, not meeting his gaze. "Loving someone doesn't automatically mean you're compatible. Sometimes, relationships just don't work out."

He didn't invade her privacy by asking for specifics. Why bother, when she'd confirmed what he already knew? Though a noble goal, happy endings were rare. Otherwise, Jim and his wife wouldn't be divorced now. Grayson's mother wouldn't have left his father. Violet's own father, Grandpa Duncan, wouldn't have had to bury his wife and stillborn son after she died during childbirth. And Blaine and Miranda…

Grayson spent a lot of time in his truck alone, and sometimes those drives turned contemplative. It had struck him more than once as a shame that Violet, who had so much love to give, hadn't found anyone special. But maybe she was too smart to open herself up to that. Why risk it? She set her own hours doing a job she loved, cultivated an active role in her community and owned three dogs who adored her unconditionally.

Not a bad life, all in all. Especially when it included brownies.

Chapter Five

"Can we come, too?" Tyler asked.

Grayson chuckled. "Sorry, but that's not usually how a date works."

"What's a date?" Sam asked, dragging a shovel behind him as he joined them at Grayson's truck.

"You have a *date*?" Tyler sounded disgusted.

With an impatient sigh, his brother repeated his question. "What is a date?"

"It's where grown-ups kiss," Tyler said.

Violet, planting tomatoes in the raised garden bed, halfheartedly smothered a laugh.

"There's not going to be any kissing," Grayson assured everyone. "I'm just taking Miss Hadley to lunch to thank her for being a job reference. But first I have to swing by the school and drop off your medical forms and records so that you two can go to kindergarten." He'd questioned whether to even enroll them, with so little time left in the school year, but it would be nice if they made a friend or two before summer vacation.

"Aw, man." Tyler kicked a rock. "Why do we hafta

go to school? I like it here. With the dogs and the dirt and Violet's cookies."

"The dogs and dirt and cookies will be here when you get home from school each day," Grayson said firmly. "But everyone has work to do. I have to get a job because I'm an adult, and you two have to go to class because you're kids. Now be good for Violet while I'm gone. Help her plant lots of healthy vegetables for us to eat."

Tyler made a face.

"You need vegetables to grow up big and strong," Grayson added.

Sam craned his head back, eyeing him. "Did *you* eat lotsa vegetables?"

Another muffled snort of laughter from his aunt.

"Hey," he grumbled, "a little support here?" Truthfully, he was relieved by her amusement. She seemed in much better spirits today than she had been last night.

As he climbed into the truck, he heard Tyler tell his brother suspiciously, "I don't think Grayson ate his vegetables."

Grayson made a mental note to have a salad with lunch so he could return with tales of nutritional virtue.

The town had changed so little over the years that driving to the school was like traveling in time. When he passed the road that led to his old house, a sharp punch of conflicted feelings hit him all at once. Before his mom left when he was seven, there'd been happy family memories. Normal kid stuff like birthdays and Christmases and learning to ride a bike in the driveway and blowing bubbles in the yard while his mother sang. But all of those memories were buried beneath the bitterness and unanswered questions that came with her abandonment. And, later, the stark terror he'd felt when a policeman and neighbor lady came to tell him about his father. Came to tell him he had no parents left.

He wrenched himself out of the painful memories. Yesterday, he'd vowed to be more positive. *No more dwelling on the past.*

Of course, that was easier said than done when he parked outside the same school he'd attended from kindergarten to fifth grade. Aside from newer playground equipment out by the bus lanes, it looked exactly as he remembered. How many times had he strolled along this very sidewalk in line with his classmates? He reached for the door, frowning when it turned out to be locked.

He tried the door next to it, with the same result. A staticky voice asked, "Can I help you, sir?" and he noticed the intercom panel. Well, that was a new addition.

"I'm dropping off some enrollment papers," he said, not sure where to look when addressing a disembodied voice.

"One moment." There was a click to signal the door was now unlocked.

He stepped inside, turning left into the main office.

The woman behind the desk nodded in greeting. "For future reference, just press the buzzer when you need to visit the school. We keep the doors locked for the children's safety."

A depressing necessity. How was he going to explain, as Tyler and Sam got older, all the bad things that lurked in the world? There were other explanations that would fall to him, too. Like the sex talk. And Santa not being real. Probably not in that order. The responsibilities ahead were dizzying.

"Sir?" The woman eyed him as though maybe she'd made a mistake letting him into the building. "You said you had enrollment papers?"

"Oh, right."

She went through the thick manila folder that included immunization records, documents from the boys' last school, proof of Grayson's new Cupid's Bow address and legal forms naming him the twins' guardian. He felt bizarrely proud of himself when she deemed everything in order. She offered him a seat while he waited for the school counselor.

Moments later, a freckled blonde who only stood as high as his shoulder introduced herself as Ms. Epperman. "But the kids call me Miss Tina." She explained that, while there were two kindergarten classes, she and the teachers had decided to put the boys in the same class to ease their nerves about not knowing anyone. "If they're nervous about anything here, I'm always available to talk. That offer extends to you, too," she said gently. "It's part of my job to discuss concerns with parents and I know this can't be an easy situation for you."

"No, ma'am." Her sympathy made him feel itchy and claustrophobic. He was glad when they left her office. She gave him a tour of the school that included a cafeteria that smelled strongly of fish sticks and a small library, which made him think fondly of Hadley and her poetry display.

The closer it got to their lunch date, the more he looked forward to seeing her again. *For the third day in a row.* That was more often than he'd seen some of the women he'd slept with.

Miranda's accusation echoed in his head. "I say this with love, but you're a coward when it comes to dating."

"I am not," he'd protested. "It's just difficult to settle into a relationship when you're on the circuit."

"Pathetic excuse. Blaine made it work with me back when he was still riding."

"Yeah, well, your husband is special."

At that, her expression had softened, all criticism of Grayson's love life forgotten. "He certainly is."

"Mr. Cox?" The guidance counselor peered up at him with concern. "Everything okay?"

"I…got distracted thinking about lunch." He gave her an apologetic smile. "Guess I'm hungrier than I realized."

"Good thing we've finished with the tour then."

They said their goodbyes, and he headed back to the truck, feeling as if he was being accompanied by ghosts.

Would there come a day when memories of Miranda and Blaine grew less common, less vibrant? He wasn't sure if he looked forward to that day or dreaded it.

HADLEY GRITTED HER teeth at the trio of women hanging around the circulation desk. Normally, she was thrilled to have patrons in the library, but she couldn't help feeling these women were here for a reason other than books. Although her friend Kate Trent regularly brought her stepdaughters in for reading material, they were both at school now. According to Kate, she and her infant daughter were meeting her mother-in-law for lunch and had just stopped in to say hi…the very day that Hadley was expecting her own lunch date to walk through the door. Next to Kate were cousins Anita and Irene Drake. Anita leaned against the counter without even trying to be subtle, glancing from the clock on the wall to the doorway.

Hadley glared at the back of Anita's head. "Don't you know a watched entrance never boils?" *Why did I ever mention that I'm going out with Grayson?*

But she was afraid she knew the answer to that. When she'd arrived to book club last night, she'd been irate over a phone call yesterday evening. One of her old softball teammates had called to say she would be able to make the ten-year reunion after all and the woman had been a little too pitying about the fact Hadley hadn't gone away to college like some of their friends. Hadley hung up feeling defensive about her life. Next weekend, she'd be hanging out with former classmates who'd married and were starting families, people who'd moved to other states and, in at least one case, another country.

And here I remain, the local librarian. No kids, no husband, no boyfriend. Hell, she didn't even have a cat.

It was a little depressing, coming on top of a week where one of her friends had called her the Quiet One and her older sister had said she needed to work on her confidence. So she'd bragged to her friends that she'd invited a sexy cowboy to lunch. Technically, he'd invited her...but only after she put the idea in his head. That had to count for something.

She cleared her throat. "I'm officially kicking you all out."

"What?" Kate looked startled.

"You heard me. Either scatter and go find some books or go home. My life is not a spectator sport."

Kate sighed. "Okay, okay." She glanced down at the baby sleeping in a sling she wore across the front of her body. "I should get to the restaurant anyway before she wakes up hungry. I can't feed her while driving. Call me later with details, though?"

"It's a friendly lunch with a guy I went to school with. How exciting are you expecting the details to be?"

"You're a natural-born storyteller," Kate said. "All anecdotes you share are exciting."

That mollified Hadley more than it should. She bit back a smile. "Suck-up."

The Drake cousins were more reluctant to go. Instead of following Kate outside, Irene suddenly remembered a book she wanted to look for, and Anita volunteered to help her find it. Hadley rolled her eyes, but at least she'd rid herself of an audience…except for blue-haired Bunny Neill, the woman who'd hired her and filled in for her on a part-time basis.

Bunny grinned, her eyes crinkling mischievously behind her tortoiseshell glasses. "Can't kick me out, dear. I work here. So, is this lunch buddy of yours the same man Alma saw you with at the grocery store?" At Hadley's nod, Bunny's grin widened. "Good for you. Alma said he was—"

"Grayson!" Hadley waved hello across the counter, silencing her predecessor before she said anything too embarrassing. "Right on time. I'm starving." He'd texted that morning to say he hoped barbecue was okay because the Smoky Pig was one of the things he'd missed most about Cupid's Bow. Since Tuesdays were her sister's day off, Hadley had readily agreed.

Purse in hand, she hurried around the counter to join him. She probably looked overeager, but she wanted to hustle him out of here before the Drake cousins returned and interrogated him. Bunny was hot on her heels, reaching over to shake his hand.

"I'm Bunny Neill." She sized him up with a nod. "Alma was right, you *are* a strapping fellow."

His eyebrows rose at this observation, but he smiled hesitantly. "Grayson Cox. Nice to meet you."

Hadley gently pried her mentor away. "We'll be back in an hour, Bunny."

"You kids take your time," Bunny called after them.

"I remember what young love is like. Why, Herbert and I used to fog up the windows of his—"

Hadley shoved the door open and practically dragged Grayson outside.

He grinned teasingly. "Hey, I didn't get to hear what Herbert drove. Car? Truck? Maybe one of those vintage '51 Ford pickups."

"Sure, make jokes. You have no idea what I just saved us from. Bunny seems to find retirement liberating. In the past year, she's taken oversharing to a new level." Hadley was emotionally scarred from Bunny reminiscing about her honeymoon.

As they reached the end of the sidewalk, Grayson asked, "Mind if I drive?"

"Go right ahead. I'm a terrible driver. I mean, not literally, but my mind wanders sometimes. I swear I get my best ideas behind the wheel. I'll be toodling along, then come up with the perfect plot twist and—"

"Plot twist?" He opened the passenger-side door for her.

"Oh. I, um, write stories." Now that she'd had a few pieces published, it was no longer a secret, but she still felt weird talking about it, as if she might jinx her future success. Plus, people's follow-up questions were sometimes uncomfortably bizarre. The manager at the movie theater had asked if the short story about a woman who methodically killed four husbands was inspired by Hadley's real life.

Still, people at her reunion were going to ask what she'd been up to, and she was proud of the stories she'd had in magazines, so she might as well practice talking about it. When Grayson got into the truck, she said, "I've only sold short stories so far, but I'm working on a book-length manuscript set in London."

"That's great. With all those reports you used to give on faraway places, I wouldn't have been surprised to come back and learn you'd become a famous travel writer. Or one of those people who blogs about hidden attractions tourists don't know about."

Her laugh was brittle. "Ironic, since I've never been outside Texas—not that there isn't lots to do in this big ol' state, but…"

"So what kind of book are you writing?"

A week ago, she could have answered that question, but for the last few days, when she sat at the keyboard, her story seemed to be pulling her in different directions, completely disregarding her careful outline. "You're sweet to show an interest, but me swearing at my computer and hitting Delete a lot isn't that exciting. Hardly the adrenaline rush of, say, bull-riding."

"You've heard about my rodeo wins?"

"Heard about, did some light internet stalking. Potato, po-tah-to." She cast him a sidelong glance. "You set some impressive records."

He smiled wistfully. "I'm sure someone else will break them soon enough. My rodeo days are behind me. I've been lucky as far as injuries go, but with the boys depending on me, it's wiser to minimize my risks."

"Will you miss it?"

"Sometimes. I loved it, but life on the circuit was

grueling. It might be nice to stay in one place for a little bit. Even if that place is Cupid's Bow."

"Hey!" She felt as if she should stick up for her hometown, but she knew he must be haunted by bad memories here. It couldn't have been easy for him to come back, and she admired that he'd done what he thought best for his adopted sons.

"At least the barbecue here is great," he conceded as they reached Main Street.

The Smoky Pig did a thriving lunch business.

Observing the stream of people entering the restaurant, Grayson asked, "Think we'll even be able to get a table?"

"You'd be surprised. Half the people coming in are picking up to-go orders, and the Boyd family—the owners—made efficient use of the space inside. I'm always impressed by how many diners they can seat. Plus, there are tables on the covered patio out back."

Sure enough, it only took the hostess a few minutes to find them a table. And the waitress materialized with superhuman speed. *You have got to be kidding.* Hadley stared at her sister, kicking herself for ever telling anyone about her lunch plans.

Ignoring Hadley's telepathic promises of retribution, Leanne smiled at Grayson. "Well, hi there! We haven't met. I'm—"

"Leanne Lanier," Hadley said. "My sister. Who doesn't work on Tuesdays."

Leanne's expression was all innocence. "Someone called in sick."

"Uh-huh. I'm going to need a name. And a signed doctor's note."

"I see your imagination has taken a turn toward paranoia," Leanne scolded lightly. "Because I love you, I'll overlook that and bring you a sweet tea and a brisket plate."

It was Hadley's favorite thing on the menu. Plus, the sooner they concluded ordering, the sooner her sister would stop intruding on her lunch. "Fine."

Across the table, Grayson added, "I'm Grayson, by the way. You can make that two teas and brisket combos. Oh, and a side salad, please."

As her sister walked away, Hadley huffed out a breath. "Wonder which one of them will report back to my mother first—Leanne the snoop or Bunny the oversharer. Honest to heaven, you'd think I'd never had lunch with a man before."

"We should do something scandalous to give them a better story."

Her gaze snapped back to him, her face heating as her imagination supplied several scenarios for scandal with Grayson. "L-like what?"

"No clue. I was just talking off the top of my head. You have any ideas?"

"Not a one," she lied, willing her cheeks to cool.

"I gather it's been a while since you…lunched with anyone?"

"Mom says I'm too picky."

He made a derisive sound low in his throat.

"What the hell did that mean?"

"You weren't 'too picky' to date Reggie George.

Sorry. I know it's none of my business, but the two of you in high school? I never got it."

She'd known Grayson and her former flame didn't exactly see eye-to-eye, but she was surprised by the hostility in Grayson's voice all these years later. "Boy, you really don't like him, huh?"

"After my mom left, he made second grade a living hell for me, and didn't let up until graduation—although he got better at disguising it to avoid detention."

Hadley frowned, comparing Grayson's description to the boy she'd known. "He could be obnoxious sometimes." Especially with his friends, who egged him on. "But I saw a different side of him. We ran in to each other at the library sophomore year, and he asked for my help with a project. He was really worried about his grade. Seeing him so vulnerable, when he wasn't trying to impress his friends, felt like a secret he'd trusted me with. And he was so grateful afterward, really sweet." Had she, the longtime bookworm mostly ignored by boys, been too ready to overlook his faults just because the popular boy had noticed her?

"We broke up shortly after graduation," she said. When she screwed up her arm, his initial sympathy had given way to impatience. He'd wanted to spend his last summer before college partying, not comforting a girlfriend whose dreams had been dashed. She darted a glance around, making sure her sister wasn't in earshot. "At the time, Leanne was in a really toxic relationship. She gave up too much of herself and was miserable. Maybe Mom's right and I did go through a 'picky' phase. But I wanted to protect myself from making a mistake. Then after Mom's stroke, I was so busy helping Daddy take care of—"

"I didn't know she had a stroke. Is she all right?"

"She is now." Thank God. Hadley had been alone with her mother when it happened, and it had been the scariest day of her life. "She has some lingering balance issues, and her speech still slurs when she's tired, but she's doing so much better." Despite her mother's successful recovery, there was a tremor in Hadley's voice when she discussed it.

"You're close to your folks, aren't you?" His pensive expression was hard to read. Was he missing his own parents?

"Yes. The silver lining of—"

"Sorry the drinks took so long." Leanne appeared with their sweet teas. "Crazy-busy lunch rush. But your food will be up in just a sec."

True to her word, she returned quickly with their plates. Grayson inhaled deeply, groaning in a low rumble of pleasure. He took a bite, closing his eyes for a second to savor it.

"Can I stay," Hadley asked, "or do you and the brisket need a moment alone?"

He grinned sheepishly. "Damn this is good."

"Agreed. Maybe one day I will see the world—or at least Colorado—but I can't imagine finding better barbecue anywhere."

"What's in Colorado?"

"A picturesque little bookshop. The owner was inspired by a place he visited in Paris, where they offer a writer-in-residence spot to aspiring authors who agree to work on their craft a certain number of hours a day and also agree to shifts in the store. He set up a similar program. There's a committee of five people, and they pick two writers a year. The shop actively participates in several literary festivals, so if you're selected, there's some nice publicity. Leanne convinced me to send in my work for consideration. It's a total long shot."

"You never know. The committee has to pick *someone*. Why not you?"

"Spoken like a reasonable person who doesn't suffer from irrational self-doubt."

"Don't bet on it. Since the boys came to live with me, I've had plenty of experience with self-doubt."

"How are they settling in?"

"So far, so good—Vi is the most nurturing person I know—but they're not looking forward to school next week. I was registering them with the administration office before I came to pick you up."

"You know, if they're apprehensive, they might find your presence reassuring. If you can manage it once or twice, volunteer to chaperone a class party or a field trip. Or just go in to be mystery reader one afternoon."

"Mystery reader?"

She nodded. "Most of the younger grades have a 'special guest' come in every other week to read a story. Sometimes it's a local official, like the mayor or the sheriff, but it's usually a class parent. The kids get a kick out of trying to guess who it will be, and you'd only be there a few minutes."

"I'll look in to it. Thanks, Hadley."

It was stupid that his saying her name curled her toes. It was just her name. People said it all the time. But Grayson's voice, combined with the grateful look he was giving her…

A full second passed with their gazes locked, no one saying anything, and Hadley found it thrilling.

From the way Grayson suddenly jerked back with a frown, he did not. "I appreciate any school advice you have for making this easier on the boys. They're my priority. My top priority," he said with emphasis. "I'm sure rodeo won't be the only thing I have to give up."

"Dating, you mean?" The twinge of disappointment she felt was idiotic. Hadn't she predicted exactly that to Leanne?

He nodded. "It was difficult enough to fit around my schedule when I was just a bull rider. But now that I'm a… Now that I have bigger responsibilities," he amended.

Obviously, he was still trying to adjust to the idea of being a parent. She didn't blame him. She kept her voice light, hoping to erase some of the tension in his gaze. "When you go to school PTA meetings, you should probably bring Violet with you. As soon as the single moms get a load of you—and how great you are with the twins—you'll need a human shield to ward off play dates and welcome-to-town casseroles."

His dimples appeared. "Are you saying I'm irresistible?"

She couldn't help grinning back. "Let's just say, if you go to the reunion Saturday, I don't think you'll have any trouble keeping your dance card full."

"Reunion?"

"Our high school's ten-year reunion. This weekend. Didn't you know?" She knew his mind had been on more important matters recently, but class representatives had been sending out social-media notices for months. Had he really not stayed in touch with anyone from their past?

He ran a hand through his hair. "Ten years? Wow. That went fast."

"Yep. An entire decade." She tried to quell the sense that she should have more to show for it.

"Doubt I'll make the reunion," he said.

"Well, I'll be there. If you change your mind, come say hi."

"I appreciate it, but the past… I'd rather focus on the here and now, trying to make a life for me and the boys."

"How's the job hunt going?"

"I have a few leads—construction's the most promising—but nothing that will allow me to get a place of my own anytime soon. Aunt Vi has done so much for me. I hate feeling like I'm taking advantage of her kindness."

"She doesn't see it that way. The reason people knew about you coming back was because she told friends. She was excited. You're her family."

"Her only family," he agreed grimly. "Unless you count my mother, which I don't. She didn't even come back for my grandfather's funeral. Hell, maybe she didn't even know about it, but Vi could have used the moral support."

He reached for his sweet tea. "Sometimes I think the very things about Cupid's Bow that make me crazy are why Violet loves it here. I hated that when my mom left, when my dad died, everyone knew. Pity and speculation were inescapable. But Vi seems to take sanctuary in the sense of community. Like she's created her own extended family."

Hadley understood. "I have a love-hate-love relationship with the place myself. When I got my softball scholarship, I felt like the whole town was proud of me. And when that fell through, I felt like I'd let people down. I've often thought about how liberating it must be to live in a big city, where I could be anonymous. On the other hand, so many friends and neighbors pitched in when Mom was in the hospital." There was that tremor in her voice again. She swallowed. "Plus, I love my job. When folks come into the library, I already know what to recommend, what they'll enjoy. I like the familiarity, the sense that I have a purpose."

"Well, I can't speak for all the library patrons, but I know those dinosaur books you sent home with us made two little boys very happy. Thank you."

She beamed at him. "There might be one other thing I can do for you, nonlibrary-related. My friend Sierra is getting married in a couple of months, and her fiancé is Jarrett Ross. You know him? He was a year ahead of us in school and a rodeo champ after that."

"Our paths have crossed once or twice. He dropped off the circuit, what…two years ago?"

"He quit competing to help run his family's ranch, but now that he's planning a wedding, he might be able to use some backup. It wouldn't be a full-time gig, but it could help you save up."

"Couldn't hurt to ask. And I miss being around horses. If I make a good enough impression, I could even talk to him about discounted riding lessons for the boys." His smile was bittersweet. "Their dad had planned to teach them eventually."

Leanne approached the table. "How's everything over here?" It was a perfectly normal question for a waitress to ask, but the way she peered at Hadley implied she was inquiring about more than the food.

This is the thanks I get for helping her with biology? "We're fine." *Go away.*

"Save any room for dessert?"

Grayson's eyes lit up. "I always have room for dessert."

"How about we give up our table here," Hadley suggested, "and walk down to Howell's Bakery? Bunny likes it when I bring her back cinnamon rolls." As a bonus, Hadley didn't have any nosy relatives that worked at the bakery.

"Fine by me," Grayson agreed.

Leanne scowled but rallied quickly. "I'll be right back with the check."

Buzzing came from inside Hadley's purse, and she pulled out her cell phone. "Speaking of Bunny… If she's interrupting lunch, she probably has a computer question." The woman knew the library like the back of her hand but was still struggling with last week's software update. "Hey, Bunny. Hang on a sec." To

Grayson, she said, "Mind if I step outside, where there's less background noise?"

"Go right ahead. I'll pay and join you in a minute."

"Okay. Dessert's on me," she said as she climbed out of the booth.

"Sorry to interrupt your hot date," Bunny said once Hadley was outside. "It's this dang computer again."

"Good. I mean, not good that the computer's giving you trouble. But I'm glad you aren't calling for some stupid reason like asking about my date."

"Of course not. I'm a professional. Besides, I plan to grill you about that when you get back."

GRAYSON HAD NOTICED a few heads turn as Hadley walked outside; some people seemed to be speculating on their lunch date. But there were a couple of cowboys who were just plain appreciating the view. He'd had the oddly possessive urge to stomp over to their table and demand, "What the hell are you looking at?" Except he knew. They were enjoying the swish of Hadley's hips in that dress. She had a gorgeous body, curvy and soft but still hinting at her athletic past.

She was undeniably enjoyable to look at. But more than that, she was enjoyable period. Aside from his aunt or the Stowes, he couldn't remember the last time he'd found it so easy to talk to someone.

"You know, if you want to tip me a little extra, I could be bribed to put in a good word for you."

Grayson whipped his head around to find Leanne grinning at him. How long had she been standing there with the bill while he sighed over her sister?

He cleared his throat. "Happy to tip the waitress who brought me the best food I've had in years, but there's no point in singing my praises to her. Hadley and I are just old classmates. Friends. I'm not looking for anything more."

"But the two of you looked so… Are you sure? My sister is the best person I know."

"She's terrific," he agreed. "My hands are just a little full right now."

From the sudden sympathetic gleam in her eyes, he knew she'd heard about the boys. He quickly handed her a few bills. "Keep the change." Then he was on the move, away from any questions about his new status as a single dad or further suggestions that he pursue Hadley romantically. Cupid's Bow—home of world-famous barbecue and unsolicited opinions.

"Bryant?" A silver-haired man in his path stopped and stared, slack-jawed. But he shook his head almost immediately. "Apologies. Bryant Cox is dead, of course. But you are the spitting image of him. Grayson?"

Shifting his weight, Grayson nodded uncomfortably. In most of his memories, his father had bloodshot eyes and a furious scowl twisting his features. It had never occurred to him that they looked alike.

"It has been too long, son. Ned Garcia. I worked at the store with Bryant, remember? You may not recognize me with all the wrinkles and gray hair." He patted his head. "But at least I have the hair. Many of my friends have gone bald."

Ned Garcia? One of the two men who'd pushed

Bryant out of his own store? After a displaced Bryant took a shift at a bottling plant outside of town, his only interactions with Ned had been blatantly hostile. Grayson remembered some shouting on the front lawn and at least one finger gesture. *What am I supposed to say? Nice to see you? Screw over any business partners lately?*

"Congratulations on keeping your hair," Grayson said stiffly. "I don't mean to be rude, but there's a lady outside waiting for me, so..."

"Go, go. But you come by the store soon and see me, okay?"

That was about as likely as lying down in the middle of a stampede for a nap. "Have a nice day, Mr. Garcia." Grayson strode away from the older man and from the ugly memories of his father's face contorted in rage as he railed that the people in this town were out to get him. A lot of those people still stood between Grayson and the door.

Lunch had been spectacular, the food even surpassing his memories, but without the buffer of Hadley's company, he felt overwhelmed by the crowd. Who else here knew him, associated him with his drunken father? *Next time you get a craving for barbecue, do yourself a favor and get takeout.*

Chapter Six

Apparently, Grayson decided during dinner, *I need to work on my poker face.* Hadley had asked him on the way back to the library if he was okay and when he'd said yes, she'd frowned with obvious skepticism. And Aunt Vi had asked him the same question twice this evening.

Truthfully, the day had left him drained—meeting with the school counselor, running in to Ned Garcia, having lunch with Hadley. Lunch had actually been a highlight but the unabashed curiosity of people like Bunny and Leanne was grating. He was already a man skeptical about happy endings, but romance in Cupid's Bow would be even harder. People would hear about a couple's every date and fight.

He wasn't very hungry, but he made an attempt to eat, wanting to set a good example for the boys and reassure Vi that he was fine. When he felt like he'd made a suitable effort, he set down his fork and turned to the boys. "Sometime this week, we should go shopping for school supplies." Their mother had loved to shop, called it therapeutic.

The boys had not inherited this trait.

"It's bad enough we hafta go to school soon," Tyler wailed. "Now we hafta go to *stores*?"

His brother was more succinct. "Blech."

"It doesn't have to be a bummer," Grayson said. "We can do something fun while we're out. We could go to the park. Or get dessert at the bakery."

"Or go to the library?" Sam asked. "I wanna get more dinosaur books. And one 'bout space. There's lotsa stars at night, and Violet says they make concentrations."

"Constellations," she said, correcting him as she began clearing away empty plates. "That's a great idea, Sammy. Bring home a book or two about the constellations, and I'll look through the garage for binoculars. I know there's a pair around here somewhere. A telescope would be even better, but…"

Grayson's cell phone rang. It was a local number. "This could be about the construction job."

"You take that," Vi said, "and I'll get the boys' bath started."

Twenty minutes later, the boys were putting on pajamas and Grayson was gainfully employed. At least for the time it took to rebuild an old church. The man who'd hired him wanted to use this project as a trial run and they could renegotiate for something more permanent if everyone was happy with how it went.

"I start Friday," he told Vi as the twins brushed their teeth. "You're sure you don't mind staying with the boys all day? Your work—"

"It's one day. Next week, they start school. I'll just

plan to be really productive until they get home at three, then run my errands with them in tow."

He winced, thinking of the cereal-aisle fiasco and the scattered books in the children's library. "You sure that's a good idea? Those boys may have a real future in the field of demolition."

She laughed. "You were a rambunctious little boy once, too, but the town's still standing."

Tyler padded into the hall, his expression perplexed. "What's ramb…"

"Rambunctious," Vi repeated slowly. "It means lively and high-spirited. But someone who gets in trouble a little, too."

"And Grayson used to get in trouble?" Tyler asked.

"A few times," she said. "No one's perfect, but he was a good boy."

No, I wasn't. In a town where people had so much intimate knowledge of each other, it was a minor miracle he'd ever gotten away with graffiti and shoplifting. He'd been petty and destructive, and if he could take it all back now…

"Done," Sam declared, joining them in the hall. He smiled broadly, showing off his sparkling teeth.

"Excellent job," Vi said. She kissed each boy on the head and told them good-night.

As Grayson tucked them in, he told them about his tour of the school. "It's nice. You'll like it there. I'm sure you'll make lots of friends."

Sam yawned. "Did you make lotsa friends in school?"

"I…" Lying seemed like bad parenting, but he didn't

want to get in to his bleak childhood. Especially not at bedtime. "Miss Hadley was in my class."

"Oh." Sam exchanged a sleepy smile with his brother, and Tyler nodded, silently agreeing that a school where Miss Hadley attended couldn't be too bad. The boys really liked her.

Thinking of her generous heart and musical laugh, Grayson decided the boys had excellent taste.

When he emerged from the room, he found Vi working on the couch with her feet on the coffee table and flanked by two dogs. The third was in bed with the twins. "I talked to Jim McKay," she said without looking up from the laptop screen. "We're all set and meeting this weekend to discuss his website. If I seemed antsy about it last night, it's only because he caught me off-guard. Blast from the past, old memories. But I'm a professional."

Grayson sat in the battered armchair she refused to get rid of because it had been her dad's favorite. "I had a different kind of blast-from-the-past encounter today."

"Talking to Hadley about old times?"

He shook his head. "I ran in to Ned Garcia and he chatted me up like we were old friends. I couldn't believe his nerve."

"Hold on, Gray. Ned's a good man."

"He and that Drake guy stole my dad's shop out from under him!" The tack-and-supply store had been started by Bryant's family; Grayson's mom got a job as a clerk there when she'd been nineteen. Bryant had been a decade older but claimed it was love at first sight. They'd married a week after Rachel's twentieth birthday, and Grayson had come along six months later.

"Ned and Albert Drake invested in that store to help your dad save it when he couldn't get a loan," Violet explained.

"Yeah, giving them majority ownership. From what I heard, it was a hostile takeover."

With a heavy exhale, she set aside her laptop. "We don't talk much about your father because I've never really known what to say."

And because Grayson had habitually changed the subject.

"I don't want to speak ill of the dead," she continued. "But after Rachel left, your father was angry at the world, and he watched events unfold from inside a bottle. His perspective was skewed."

Grayson couldn't argue with those facts. Still, Ned and Albert *had* taken control of the store. That was indisputable.

"After you came to live with me, Ned periodically sent me checks to help out—although he didn't want any fuss and got embarrassed when I thanked him."

"Maybe he sent the money out of guilt."

"He sent it because he cared. There was a time when he and your dad were close friends. He tried to get Bryant to AA meetings."

"He did?" Grayson couldn't help wondering, just for a second, how life might've been different if Ned had succeeded.

"Albert Drake passed away last winter, so it's just

Ned running the store now. The place mostly sells ranch and riding supplies, but he special-orders me dog food at a discount."

The picture she painted of a kindly man who'd gone out of his way to try to help a doomed friend was something he would have to ponder. It didn't fit the narrative he'd been told—but was he really going to trust a bitter drunk over Aunt Vi? "Speaking of ranches, I may have a line on a second job."

She laughed. "That was fast. You haven't even started the first job."

"You know the Twisted R?"

"The Ross spread, yeah. They hosted the Harvest Day Festival there a year or two ago."

He rolled his eyes. "Cupid's Bow and its town celebrations. Harvest Days, the Sweetheart Festival, the Centennial Trail Ride, the Hey-it's-a-Wednesday-in-March Festival..."

"The Centennial celebration, by definition, is only once every hundred years. You can't count it." She grinned. "But I'll be happy to bring up your Wednesday-in-March idea at the big town meeting this Friday."

"Big town meeting?"

She nodded. "Town hall, followed by a movie under the stars. Everyone I know is planning to go. Want to join me?"

Not even a little bit. "After a day of working construction, I'll probably hit the shower and fall face-down in bed."

"The movies are always family-friendly. I can take the boys if you're thinking of turning in early."

"You're the best."

"That's what my Greatest-Aunt-in-the-World mug tells me. But reminders are always appreciated, too."

THERE WAS NOTHING like soaking in a perfect Texas day from atop a horse. The sun was bright, yet not punishing, and bluebonnets flourished along the trail. Even if Jarrett Ross decided not to offer him part-time work, Grayson deemed this an afternoon well spent. He'd called the man that morning and discovered that Hadley had already put in a good word for him.

Now, he and Jarrett were approaching the stable, having concluded their tour of the ranch. "That's pretty much the whole operation," Jarrett said as he dismounted. "Any questions?"

"No, but it sure was good to ride again. I hadn't realized how much I missed it." He was used to ranching odd jobs that kept him in the saddle when he wasn't on the circuit, and he'd had a standing invitation to a friend's stables back when he'd lived in his trailer. Grayson did some of his best thinking on horseback. "I've been considering signing up the boys for lessons." Maybe after he got his first paycheck.

They led the horses inside. "I met their dad a few times," Jarrett said. "Blaine Stowe? He was a good guy."

"Best friend I ever had."

"I competed against him in Fort Worth once. Kicked my ass," Jarrett said with a grin. "When he quit riding, I didn't know whether to be relieved or ticked off that he retired before I had a chance to beat him."

Grayson had to laugh at that. "Probably a lot of guys out there feel the same way about you."

"Maybe a few. My family went through a rough time, though, and I needed to be here. I don't miss the circuit like I thought I might. Hell, if things had been different, I never would have met Sierra. The way my fiancée tells it, moving back to Cupid's Bow wasn't your first choice, but keep an open mind." He inhaled deeply, the picture of contentment. "Life here can be pretty perfect sometimes."

"I'm not holding my breath for perfect. I'm just trying to get by."

"Well, the part-time job is yours if you want it. I need a person to take over some of the weekend riding lessons temporarily to free me up for premarital counseling at the church and a couple of trips we have planned to Houston. That's where Sierra's family lives."

"I'd love to help. Thank you."

"Glad it worked out. Any friend of Hadley's is a friend of ours."

Friend. She was, wasn't she? She'd been encouraging about the boys, she was fun to talk to, she was even the person who'd given him the tip about contacting Jarrett. But if someone had asked him a month ago how he remembered Hadley, he would have had a hazy recollection of a know-it-all honor-roll student who sucked up to teachers and was blindly loyal to her crappy boyfriend. What was it Vi had said about Grayson's father? He had a skewed perspective.

So did I. Grayson had never considered Hadley a

potential friend when he lived here, and he'd been wrong. He'd thought Ms. Templeton had been out to get him, and he'd been wrong. He'd bought in to his dad's characterization of Ned Garcia as a cheating opportunist, and, according to Vi, he'd been wrong.

If he did as Jarrett advised and kept an open mind about Cupid's Bow, would he discover that he'd grossly misjudged others, too? It was disorienting, to have his long-held cynicism about the town challenged. But Sam and Tyler lived here now. He'd much rather they grow up in the place Jarrett and Hadley and Vi loved than the place he'd once believed it to be.

WHAT AM I DOING? Theoretically, Grayson was on a *kolache* run. He'd told Violet he would pick up breakfast Thursday morning at the Czech bakery on the other side of town. Yet he'd detoured into a neighborhood he only vaguely remembered from his teen years.

He hadn't slept well last night, had been plagued by his conscience. Every day he was in Cupid's Bow, the more he regretted the actions of this past. The conversation he and Vi had about his father's toxic anger had reminded him of the loan officer Grayson had resented for turning down his dad. He'd destroyed the man's mailbox.

Now here he was, back in the cul-de-sac where he'd gotten away with property damage. He hadn't quite worked out what he was planning to say or do. It was about twelve years too late to buy a replacement mailbox—assuming the loan officer still lived here. Grayson only knew that his past actions were troubling him and, unless he took some action in the present, he had a lot of sleepless nights ahead.

Cupid's Bow was surrounded by small farmhouses, like Vi's, and larger ranches. But closer to the quaint downtown district were subdivisions with matching brick homes and neatly maintained yards. The house he'd sought out wasn't as well-kept as some of the others. The wooden shutters framing the windows needed new paint, and weeds were sprouting up through the grass. The pieces of a cracked birdbath sat to the side of the driveway and the car out front could use washing.

He took the two steps onto the front porch, glad the wood seemed sturdier than the cracked shutters. Otherwise, it could be a safety hazard. Before he could talk himself out of it, he knocked twice across the front door, half-hoping no one was home.

A moment later, a rail-thin woman with bright blue eyes opened the door. She looked like she was in her sixties, about the right age for the loan officer's wife. "Are you here to haul off the birdbath?" she asked. "Let me get my wallet, so I can pay you for your time."

"No, ma'am. Although I'm happy to help you with that, unless someone else is already on his way. I'm, ah, Grayson Cox. Violet Duncan's nephew?" Mention of Violet usually put a smile on people's faces.

This woman was no exception. She gave him a tentative smile. "And what can I do for you this morning?"

He ran a hand through his hair, feeling like a fourteen-year-old hooligan about to face the principal. "Is Mr. Pembroke here? Stanley Pembroke?"

"Oh, goodness, no." She pressed a hand to her heart. "I'm Martha Pembroke. My Stanley died in January. Pneumonia."

"I'm so sorry to hear that, ma'am." What now? Had he upset her by mentioning her late husband? So much for atoning. He was making things worse.

She cocked her head, studying him. "I don't recognize you. How did you know Stanley?"

"I just moved back to Cupid's Bow this week, and Mr. Pembroke did some business with my dad once. I, uh, guess I wanted to talk to him about old times. I didn't mean to bother you. And, again, I can take this birdbath with me, if you'd like."

"No need. If you aren't the young man coming for it, then someone else should be along shortly." Her eyes dimmed. "Shame about the bath, though. I loved watching the birds. I don't know all their names—Stanley was the real ornithologist—but they sure are pretty. And so musical. Brighten up a whole day, don't they?"

In his head, he heard Hadley's laugh. "Yes, ma'am."

"Anyway, welcome back to Cupid's Bow. If you're looking to reconnect with people to talk about old times, there's a big town meeting tomorrow night. Everyone will be there."

"Thanks for the tip." He gave her a friendly wave and headed for his truck. Should he have apologized to her? It had been her mailbox, too, presumably. But he hadn't even worked out what he would've said to the loan officer, much less the man's grieving widow.

Well, he'd wronged others besides Mr. Pembroke. That wasn't something he was proud of, but it did mean there were still people out there he might be able to make amends to.

Next time, have a game plan first.

BY THE TIME they arrived at the library Thursday afternoon, Grayson needed a win. After his visit to the Pembroke house that morning, he'd spent two miserable hours shopping with the boys, and it started raining before they could swing by the park. Grayson considered himself rodeo-tough, but getting cranky five-year-olds to try on clothes could break a man. And how were they already outgrowing everything? They hadn't even been with him a month!

But now that they'd reached the library, things were looking up. He could placate the boys with some new books, then take them home for mandatory naps. Perhaps he could soften the blow of naptime by letting them fall asleep in front of a cartoon.

At the moment, however, neither boy showed signs of being half as tired as Grayson.

Sam raced on ahead, eager to find books about stars. After their discussion in the truck about library voices, he spoke in an excited whisper, his words rushing together. "Hi, Miss Hadley! We're back! I love the dinosaur books. Do you have some about con-stations? Me and Violet are gonna look at stars."

She grinned down at Sam. "We have a bunch of

books with constellations. I'll come help you find them after I get these ladies all checked out, okay?"

"What a cutie," one of the patrons in line murmured. She raised her eyes to Grayson. "Yours?"

"I, uh, yes. He is. They are." He put his hand on Tyler's shoulder, feeling both uncomfortable and proud.

"Well, if they love books that much, you must be doing something right."

God, I hope so. An hour ago, he'd been battling for patience in a department store when Sam had a meltdown over a button—the boy had furiously announced to everyone in a five-mile radius "I can't do it!" while simultaneously refusing Grayson's help. At least no muttered curse words had escaped Grayson's lips. The first week the boys had lived with him, he'd forgotten himself a dozen times.

Okay, two dozen.

He briefly met Hadley's gaze and returned her smile but kept walking so that he didn't interrupt her work.

She joined them a few minutes later. "It's great to see you all again!" She kneeled down to hug both boys. "Which one was your favorite dinosaur book?"

While she and the boys discussed iguanodons and orkoraptors, other kids began to show up—not just trickling in, but en masse.

Hadley straightened. "Almost time for the puppet show! Molly's coming in to do a story. Sometimes, she brings Trouble, too."

"Puppets?" Tyler was dubious.

"You'll like Molly. She's *very* cool." Just as Hadley was making this promise, a young woman with pink-

and-blue hair walked in, accompanied by a German shepherd on a leash.

"You can bring *dogs* into the library?" Sam gasped.

"Only certain dogs," Hadley said. "Trouble belongs to the mayor—Molly's sister—and is extremely well trained. You want to go pet her?"

Both boys happily scampered off, and Grayson couldn't help the sigh of relief that left him. "Finally—peace. How long is this puppet show? And would it be wrong to catch a nap in my truck?"

She laughed, the sound soothing his frayed nerves. "Tough day?"

"Yeah. But it's not all the boys' fault. I didn't sleep much last night. And my morning went awry. I went to see Stanley Pembroke, only to discover that he passed away a few months ago." Why was he telling her this? Granted, she was a great listener, but did he really want to admit he'd once smashed a mailbox and it had taken him over a decade to apologize?

"Oh, no." She squeezed his shoulder. "Were you two close?"

"Barely knew him. He… There was a thing, back in the day, with my dad." Pausing, he tried to collect his thoughts. "Violet's helping me find some clarity about my past, and maybe I just wanted to tell Stanley I understood why he made the decision he did."

"He was such a sweet man. The Pembroke house is down the street from my parents. I hate that Martha's all alone now. Both of her kids are grown and have moved out of state. I—" She stared over his shoulder at the clock on the wall. "Oh! We're supposed to be starting. Excuse me a second."

She made her way to the corner of the room, where a puppet booth was set up, and called for everyone's attention. Most of the moms sat on the floor with their toddlers and preschoolers. One or two hovered on the edges of the room, like Grayson. Hadley introduced Molly, thanked her for coming and told the audience to enjoy the tale of the cursed prince and the daring princess who rescued him.

Then Hadley made her way back to Grayson, stopping periodically to murmur soft hellos to some of the other parents and hug little kids. "There's a town meeting tomorrow night," she whispered.

So I hear.

"I won't be there," she said, "but—"

"What? Well, I'm not going then. If my favorite person in town isn't coming, what's the point?"

"Favorite, huh?"

"I got that part-time job with Jarrett Ross. I owe you one."

"You don't owe me anything. He needs a little help before his wedding, you need a little extra cash. I'm glad it worked out."

"So what were you saying about the town meeting?"

"You mentioned clarity about your past. If you're interested in revisiting your past, it seems like attending the reunion would be a logical step. But I know you're not interested," she said, staving off his objections. "Going to the meeting would be a less formal way of reconnecting with some former classmates and other folks who knew you when. It should be a well-attended town hall. Mayor Johnston has been drumming up enthusiasm for a number of improvements and programs. Plus, Friday is when they'll vote on the theme for this summer's Watermelon Festival."

"Wouldn't the theme, by default, be...watermelon?"

She grinned as if he'd told a joke. He really did not get this town's love of meetings and festivals. But he was developing a fondness for the town library. Even the puppet show was good. Molly was reaching her target audience—the kids—without talking down to them, and the adults were laughing in all the right places, too. Sam and Tyler were leaning forward, paying rapt attention, and he wondered if Molly ever did any babysitting.

At the show's conclusion, Hadley disappeared into the crowd, thanking families for coming and helping children find books. He didn't get a chance to talk to her again until it was his turn in line at the circulation desk.

"Why won't you be at the big Watermelon-Festival meeting?" he asked as he handed her his library card. "Don't like watermelons? Or festivals?"

"For your information, I'm a big fan of both. But I'm not a morning person. We have a shipment of books coming in and volunteers who will show up Saturday to help the process them. I'd rather stay late Friday to prep everything than have to get up at the crack of dawn Saturday."

"Reasonable." He could get up early if he had to, but he didn't enjoy waking up. Unless there was a beautiful woman pressed against him. It felt wrong to think about that with Hadley's dark eyes locked on his—wrong, but damn alluring. Clearing his throat, he looked away, his gaze landing on a coin bank shaped like a rocket ship. "Astro-Ashley Assistance Fund?"

"Ashley's an incredibly bright sixth grader. Her science-fair project is on display back there." She pointed toward a shelving unit. "It's her dream to go to Space Camp, but her parents are having a tough time affording it. So I figured, why not raise a little money on their behalf? Like you said, community is extended family. Shouldn't family be there for each other?"

He reached for his wallet and put a five-dollar bill in the bank.

"Besides—" Hadley leaned forward, her tone conspiratorial "—I've done things I'm not proud of before. Maybe giving others a boost helps balance the karmic scales."

He stared at the bank, mulling over her words. His scales needed a *lot* of balancing. Maybe making amends wasn't a matter of figuring out what to say to people a decade after the fact; maybe it was more about finding a way to quietly lend a hand here in the present.

Before, he'd done anonymous acts of destruction out of anger at this town. Perhaps the time had come for some anonymous acts of kindness.

Chapter Seven

Hadley was a quarter of the way home Friday night when she realized she should have grabbed something for dinner while she was still in the heart of town. She was officially too tired to cook. Heck, she might even be too tired to eat.

Nah, who was she kidding? She could always dredge up the energy to eat.

As she mentally catalogued the ingredients in her kitchen for the easiest meal option—did cookie-dough frozen yogurt count as a meal?—her cell phone rang. "Hello?"

"Hadley, dear? It's Mom."

Hadley grinned inwardly. Her mother always started conversations the same way, as if her daughter wouldn't recognize the voice of the woman who'd birthed and raised her. "What's up? I thought you were at the town meeting."

"We are. That's the problem. Quilting club ran late, and I didn't get a chance to go home before the meeting. I asked your father if he remembered to feed Bear and let him outside, but you know how he is."

"Dad or Bear?"

Her mother sighed. "Are you home already?"

"Nope. Just left the library a little while ago."

"Would it be a terrible inconvenience for you to stop by our house?"

Actually, it was on the way. "Can I raid the fridge for leftovers while I'm there?"

"Of course. I made a lasagna yesterday and pot roast the night before."

Hadley's mouth watered. "Then Bear will have company for dinner."

A few minutes later, she pulled in to her parents' subdivision. Bear met her at the door, slobbering affectionately. It was his usual hello. She fed the hound and microwaved some lasagna. Afterward, the two of them sat companionably on the couch and watched a sitcom.

She scratched him behind his ear. "The sad part is, you're one of the better dates I've had this year." Unless she counted lunch with Grayson, which seemed unwise. He'd made a point of telling her he wasn't interested in dating anyone.

But it was hard to remember that with the way he'd grinned at her at the library yesterday. He'd called her one of his favorite people.

Big deal. Bear is one of my *favorite people—and he's not even a person.*

As she let Bear out back one last time, she contemplated some of the other single men in Cupid's Bow. Now that her mom was doing so much better, Hadley could spare time and energy to date. Wasn't Jace Trent, the sheriff's appealing younger brother, still single?

And there was that one Breelan cousin who didn't seem to get in as much trouble as the rest of his family. Yet, as she tried to picture the men in her mind, her brain kept fixing on the image of Grayson's dimples.

Annoyed with her own lack of discipline, she stomped out of her parents' house, locking the door behind her. She had to duck beneath a tree branch that hung over the driveway and straightened just in time to see a truck pass by on the street. *Looks like Grayson's pickup.*

Oh, for pity's sake. An overactive imagination was one thing, but hallucinating the guy's truck bordered on obsession.

Except, it really did look like his truck. She stared after it, startled when the driver cut off the headlights, inching slowly toward the cul-de-sac. Why would someone do that? Granted, she was prone to flights of fancy, but purposely driving with no headlights in the dark seemed suspicious. She crept forward on the sidewalk to keep the vehicle in her line of sight; she also kept her cell phone clutched in her hand, prepared to dial 911 if necessary. She was inquisitive, not reckless.

The truck parked in front of the Pembroke house, and when the driver opened the door, the interior light came on. She squinted, disbelieving. That *was* Grayson! She almost shouted hello, but she'd need to be closer for him to hear her and if she interrupted, she might not get answers. Why was he sneaking around Martha Pembroke's house in the dead of night?

It's not even eight thirty. Okay, fine, not quite the dead of night. But this was still weird.

Her imagination began assembling a list of people who might have reason to skulk in the shadows. Superhero billionaires keeping the town safe from crime. Mafia hitmen.

Before she could think of a third, Grayson carried something up to Mrs. Pembroke's front porch. Okay, so he was delivering something for her. Nothing sinister about that. But he stayed there for a few minutes, moving in the dark. Hadley couldn't tell from this distance what the heck he was doing. Then he hopped down the steps into the yard, and she saw a thin beam of light from his phone as he kneeled down. Was he looking for something he'd dropped?

He stayed in the same place for a few minutes, then stood, walking another few feet before repeating the process. It occurred to her that if any of the neighbors saw a strange man with a flashlight, someone might call Sheriff Trent. But most of the neighbors were at the town meeting. Really, if you had criminal intent, this was the perfect time to case a joint in Cupid's Bow. But unless Grayson was stealing dandelions from the yard, she didn't think he was doing anything illegal.

She sidled closer, wishing she had Bear with her. Then she could pretend it was a coincidence to bump in to him while she was walking the dog and ask what he was doing. Would he tell her? Grayson had moments of pained silence, usually involving his late friend or guardianship of the boys, and she knew it wasn't always easy for him to open up. But whatever he was up to in Martha's yard wasn't—

Shoot! He'd darted back toward his truck. Was she

visible in the streetlight? She flattened herself against the tree and watched him slowly pull away from the curb, headlights still not on. Now that she had a full stomach and an intriguing mystery, her earlier fatigue was forgotten. She scurried back to her car. She wanted to follow him, see if he made any more bizarre stops while the citizens of Cupid's Bow were away from their homes.

I have so many questions. The sensible thing to do would probably be to call him later and ask. But when had "sensible" been any match for her curiosity?

GRAYSON UNLOCKED THE side door into Violet's kitchen, awash in conflicting emotions. Doing a couple of good deeds for others was a nice feeling, but changing a lightbulb, hanging a bird feeder and pulling some weeds hardly made up for two years of vandalism and spite. At least there was one thing he wasn't conflicted about: his need for a shower. His new boss had offered him overtime today, so Grayson had worked until almost seven, then quickly seized the opportunity to make a few stops while so many citizens were at the town meeting.

He pulled off his shirt as he passed the laundry room, then pitched it directly into the washer. He was unlacing his work boots when headlights hit the front window. Violet and the boys shouldn't be back for at least another hour; the twins had been excited about watching the movie. He frowned, thinking back to last night. Tyler had been sniffling and coughing. Since there'd been no fever and the area was currently under a high pollen alert, Grayson had assumed spring allergies. But what if he'd been wrong? What if one or both of the boys was really sick?

He hurried back out the door he'd just come through, meeting the car in front of the house. But it wasn't Violet's.

His eyes widened when Hadley Lanier climbed out of a compact car. "What are you doing here?"

"Oh, no, *I'm* asking the..." Her gaze dropped from his face and trailed over his bare chest. She swallowed. "Could I, uh, get a glass of water?"

"You drove to Aunt Vi's because you were thirsty?"

"I'm having an odd night. Not a bad one, so far, but definitely odd. Why were you at Martha's?"

"What?" He rocked back, stunned by the question. "How do you know about that?"

"I saw you drive up to her house with no lights on—"

"I was being inconspicuous."

"There's a fine line between *inconspicuous* and *shady*. You know who else goes up to houses at night while trying not to draw attention to themselves? Thieves and other criminals." She reached in her pocket. "You should know, I have Mace and can dial 911 with just the push of a button."

In the dark, he couldn't read her expression well enough to tell if she was joking. "You don't seriously think I was stealing from Martha Pembroke?" *You've stolen before*. It wasn't as if he was such an upstanding guy. "I bought her some bird feeders and hung them on her front porch." A stone birdbath equal to the one that had broken was currently outside his budget.

Hadley stared at him, looking even more perplexed than before. "You snuck up to her house in order to hang a bird feeder."

"And pulled some weeds from her yard." Mowing the lawn was out of the question in the dark. Plus, the noise would attract attention.

"I thought you said you barely knew the Pembrokes."

"Which is true. What I did wasn't about Martha, specifically. Before I went there, I changed a lightbulb on Pratt Street." It had been dark when he'd driven to work that morning, and he'd noticed one that was out. "It's more about helping. In general."

A dazzling smile broke across her face, and she took a step toward him. "You're amazing. For all your complaints about this town, you wait until everyone's busy then go—"

"Don't look at me like that. Don't paint me as some budding folk hero," he pleaded. "This isn't impressive. This is just a belated guilty conscience. When we were in high school, I did a ton of things I'm ashamed of, things I should have been punished for but I wasn't caught." By the time he'd graduated, people were so used to him being on the periphery that they no longer paid him much attention.

"Everyone makes mistakes," she said.

He continued as if she hadn't spoken. "I stole things from local stores because I was mad my dad lost his store. I spray-painted graffiti on the sidewalk in front of the church because I thought it was full of hypocrites who gossiped about each other. I stole the Durner High mascot and put it in the George family shed." He'd left an anonymous tip with the high school's front office on where the donkey could be found, hoping Reggie would take the blame. Plus, there'd been the obvious "ass" symbolism.

"You?" She pressed a hand to her midsection. His eyes had adjusted to the dark well enough for him to see the color drained from her face. "You're the reason I broke my arm and screwed up my shoulder?"

"What? What are you talking about?"

"A bunch of us were hanging out at Reggie's pool. Some of the graduating girls from the softball team wanted to paint a going-away sign for our coach. I went to the shed for supplies, and scared the donkey. He kicked. I tried to jump out of the way but lost my balance."

"Oh, God. I'm so sorry. I never meant..." For anyone to get hurt? Would his eighteen-year-old self have been sorry if Reggie was the one harmed?

"Turns out, you shouldn't brace your arm in front of you if you're falling. Especially on a cement floor, just makes the impact worse. The shelving unit that toppled over on me didn't help, either." Her voice cracked, and she sounded as if she was fighting tears. "I tore a ligament in my shoulder. After it healed, I tried to pitch again, but my shoulder tends to pop out of the socket easily now. Recurrent instability, the doctors said."

Grayson was nauseous. The idea of her in pain was like a toxin in his body that he needed to purge. "Hadley..." He didn't consciously reach for her; his hands moved of their own volition. He wanted to hold her, whisper apologies against her dark hair and beg for a way to make it up to her.

She jerked away. "I have to go."

A photograph of his dad's truck wrapped around that tree had been in the *Cupid's Bow Chronicle*. The image seared him. He didn't want her driving while she was upset. "Can I take you home?"

She shot him a withering glare.

Right. That had been a dumb-ass question. "Can I call Leanne to pick you up then?"

"I'll be fine. I just don't want to be here."

Didn't want to be anywhere near him, she meant. He didn't blame her. He deserved her contempt. "Will you at least text me when you get home, so I know you made it safe?"

She nodded tightly, climbing back into the car without saying a word.

The girl who'd wanted to see the world had lost her scholarship because he'd been so petty he'd tried to frame Reggie George for a juvenile crime. So much guilt and self-loathing surged through him that he half expected to choke on it. *I was an idiot.* Even if Reggie did get in trouble for the prank, it wouldn't have changed the years of bullying that came before. It wouldn't have brought back Grayson's mom. Or resurrected his father. It had been an empty gesture that had harmed one of the sweetest people he knew.

He staggered blindly toward the house. Basic muscle memory carried him through a shower, his mind reeling. He got shampoo in his eyes but didn't care. The second he stepped out, he reached for the phone to see if Hadley had texted. But it took another ten minutes before he got her message: I'm here.

I'm sorry, he typed back. Apologizing again felt hollow. It didn't fix anything. But he couldn't *not* apologize.

Three dots appeared, as if she was responding, but then they vanished. No answer ever came. And he supposed he deserved that, too.

HADLEY CHUCKED HER cell phone onto the couch, not wanting to exchange further messages with Grayson. Not tonight. She was too infuriated by what he'd told her. Too infuriated by the memory of his teenage self, the guy who'd rebuffed her the couple times she'd tried to reach out to him. Now, she regretted *ever* feeling bad for him. He hadn't just been some misunderstood loner having trouble finding his crowd; he'd been a mascot-stealing bastard who'd jacked with her future.

To hell with Grayson Cox.

I'm going to write. She punched the power button on her laptop, looking forward to murder. One of her characters would not survive the night. Maybe more than one.

She paced the living room while she waited for the computer to boot up and found herself pulling her favorite romance novel off the cluttered mantel. *What's with the book, Lanier?* She was enraged, not in the mood for a sentimental happy ending.

Nonsense. Calm logic came from somewhere deep

within her brain, below the churning emotions and sense of betrayal. It's always a good time for a happy ending. The world needs more happy.

Grayson Cox had needed more happiness in a childhood filled with loss and hurt. *Do not make excuses for him.* Plenty of people faced challenges without resorting to grand-theft donkey. What he did was not justified.

The house phone rang, and she jumped, dropping her book. Hardly anyone called her landline anymore, especially at this hour. She glanced at the display screen on the cordless phone. Lanier, Wanda. "Hey, Mom. Everything okay?"

"I wanted to thank you for taking care of Bear," her mother said. "Tried your cell first. Is it silly that I worried when you didn't answer? I know you're a grown woman, but with you living all alone..."

Hadley's house was outside the more expensive cluster of subdivisions in town. Her closest neighbor was half a mile away. "Sorry. I'm..." *Avoiding the good-looking cowboy who destroyed my dreams.* "Charging my cell. Didn't hear it. How was the meeting?"

"Good, good. Bunny Neill raised a few eyebrows, though, when she suggested a toga-party theme for the Watermelon Festival. I couldn't tell if she was just messing with people or if she actually thought it was a good idea. She said it reminded her of her college days."

College. Hadley's vision blurred as tears stung her eyes. She had her diploma from a much cheaper, closer university than she'd planned to attend. She'd lost her first choice just like she'd lost her ability to play ball. She'd loved softball. It had brought her out of her shell. It had brought her closer to her family; they hadn't always known how to relate to her wild imagination or her love of getting lost in a book, but they knew how to cheer like the proudest parents in the bleachers. Grayson had screwed that all up for her.

"Hadley, dear? Are you still there?"

"Sorry, Mom. Just tired, I guess. I should go—big day tomorrow with work and the reunion afterward."

"All right. Good night, then. I love you."

Hadley hung up the phone thinking about the fights she used to have with her sister when she was in grade school and Leanne was in middle school. Their mother would admonish them to forgive each other, "not for your sister's sake but for your own. Forgiveness is so much healthier than anger."

Hadley believed that. She *wanted* to forgive Grayson. She just didn't know where to start.

THE BOYS WERE asleep when Vi got home. Grayson was relieved. He couldn't bear to face the twins tonight. Being their guardian made him want to be the best possible role model—Blaine had left big boots to fill—and he'd never been more ashamed of himself than he was tonight.

He helped Vi carry in the boys. He tugged off their shoes, but let them sleep in their clothes, almost envying their soft peaceful snores. Grayson doubted he'd get a wink of sleep tonight.

"How was your first day of work?" Vi asked softly as they left the room.

Honestly, he hardly remembered a thing about his day before his confrontation with Hadley in the yard. He couldn't believe he'd hurt her. Had his actions had other repercussions he'd yet to learn about? Dread trembled through him; the time to confess had come. Would Aunt Vi ever look at him the same?

"I have to talk to you," he said haltingly.

She frowned. "Okay. You look awful. Whatever it is, we'll work through it tog—"

"I don't deserve your help." He sank onto the sofa, cradling his head in his hands. "I'm a terrible person."

She sat next to him. "That's not true."

"You don't know. When I came to live with you, after Dad died, I was so angry. I hated everyone. I hated this town, and I did stupid things. Stealing, graffiti, vandalism."

She sucked in a breath. "Then Jim was—"

He jerked his head up, startled. What did her ex-boyfriend have to do with this? "Violet?"

"Nothing." She bit her lip, her eyes troubled.

He'd never done anything to Jim. At least, not directly. "Did I hurt him somehow?"

"No. He was suspicious, though. Tried to warn me that he thought you were up to no good. But we'd been having other problems, and I thought… Well, I didn't believe him."

His stomach knotted. "Please tell me that's not why you broke up." The consequences of his actions were so much worse than he'd known. "If I hurt you, too…"

"Who did you hurt?"

"You remember how Hadley lost her scholarship because of injuries? She got hurt because of a dumb-ass prank that I pulled. I didn't know until tonight. I stole our rival school's mascot and put it in Reggie George's family shed as payback for years of torment." The irony was brutal. One of the reasons he'd hated Reggie was because he'd always been able to weasel out of getting in trouble. His father had seen to that. Reggie had never taken responsibility. Now, Grayson realized he was just as bad. Worse, maybe.

"Grayson." Vi's voice was heavy with disappointment.

"Hadley didn't know the donkey was in the shed. How could she? She startled it, it kicked, she fell into a shelving unit..." He was choking on too much regret and self-loathing to keep going. "I don't know if she'll ever talk to me again."

His aunt squeezed his hand, and the gesture of comfort left him weak with relief and humility.

"I am so sorry, Violet." His voice broke. "I was a rotten kid."

"You were a wounded kid, suffering multiple tragedies. I should have seen how—"

"Please don't blame yourself." This was what he'd feared when he came back to Cupid's Bow and first considered coming clean. He'd wanted to be honest with her, but not at the expense of hurting her. "You did the best you could to turn me into a good person."

"You *are* a good person. Hadley knows that. I have to believe that, in time, she'll forgive you. And you're not the only one who made mistakes. There's something I should tell you," she said raggedly. "Before I do, it's important that you know Jim and I, much as we loved each other, had problems before I got custody of you. He always seemed to want a little more than I could give. On the one hand, he praised me for caring about other people, but then he'd complain that I had more time for volunteering than I did for him. So we could've self-destructed even if you'd never come to live with me. But we did have a huge fight once over a lie I told you."

"A lie?" He had no trouble imagining Vi telling a fib for someone else's own good, but he couldn't think of anything big enough that it would cause a real fight.

"A lie of omission. A secret I kept." She took a deep breath. "A week after your junior year started, Rachel showed up here."

"Mom?" It was an oddly familiar word to use when he could barely picture what she looked like. "My mother came here?"

"While you were in school. She showed up at the front door in tears, said she'd only recently learned of your father's passing, cooed over my pictures of you like a proud mama. And we cried over our dad dying, too. For a moment, I thought she was going to come home, that we'd all be a family."

Family. He had so many mixed reactions to the word. It was both what he'd craved and what had always hurt him the most, with Aunt Vi as the only exception. And now he was even regarding her with wary misgivings, waiting to hear the rest of her tale.

"She finally told me about her new husband in San Antonio and mentioned that they'd been trying—unsuccessfully—to get pregnant. She didn't want to come back to Cupid's Bow, she wanted to take you with her. And you might have picked that, if I'd given you a choice, but I saw red. I was furious she might try to use you as a Band-Aid in her marriage, providing her husband with a convenient son to watch football with and take fishing. So I threw her out. The first time she left you, it was her own selfish decision. But the second time? *I* decided. I was so scared she would take you away, scared she'd hurt you all over again."

It took him a minute to find his voice. "And she just let you? You tossed her out and she went without a fight?" He was Rachel's biological son, and Vi had been young. Odds were, his married mother could have easily won a custody battle—if she'd cared enough to initiate one. Why should it sting that she hadn't? He'd known for most of his life that he wasn't a priority for the woman.

"I haven't talked to her since that day," Vi continued. "But she left a phone number. I have no idea if it's still good or not. Her new name is—or was—Rachel Nance, and San Antonio was her last known location."

All those years, wondering if his mom was hiking through the Rockies or living the beach life in Cali or off somewhere in Europe, and she'd been right here in the freaking state?

"I should have told you sooner," she said tremulously.

Probably. But, as she'd said, people make mistakes.

The difference was, her mistake came from a place of caring and trying to protect someone she loved. Grayson's had been malicious, fueled by vengeful anger. "I don't know how I would've reacted if you'd offered me the choice to go with her. But I do know, you've been there for me from the very beginning."

"You're not mad?"

"You were young and trying to do the best you could. I can relate." He glanced down the hall toward the boys' room. "I want to be better. I want to put good in the world."

What he really wanted was to take back the past, but no amount of wishing for good intentions would undo what he'd done to Hadley.

CONSIDERING THE LACK of sleep he'd gotten, it was amazing Grayson was even awake at seven in the morning, much less pulling up to the Cupid's Bow park.

Last night, he'd told Vi about his idea of doing anonymous good deeds. She was torn between approving and worrying that it counted as trespassing. "If you get busted on someone else's property," she'd said, "at least I'm on good terms with the sheriff. I did a webform for his wife so her piano students could schedule lessons online." But Violet had encouraged him to think bigger when it came to his community payback.

"You have a lot to make up for," she'd said. "Maybe you should start with teenagers making the same kind of bad decisions you made."

"You mean volunteering to supervise your mentorship program?"

"I was thinking something more immediate. There's a trio of high schoolers picking up litter at the park first thing in the morning. They were assigned community service in lieu of suspension. I was going to chaperone, but you could fill in for me. Plus, the church food pantry can always use volunteers to sort through donations and weed out expired goods. But do you know what I think would be *really* fitting penance for you?" She'd grinned with sudden mischief.

"I am literally afraid to ask."

"You should be on the Watermelon Festival committee!"

"A festival? Dear Lord. Anything but that."

But he knew he would give in—just as he'd agreed to be here this morning, in the parking lot with a clipboard of names and participation forms, waiting for his three felon-teers.

As a parent dropped off a surly teen with a goatee, an ancient sedan drove up and parked nearby. The kid who climbed out was built like a linebacker and all but snarled when he saw his classmate. According to the paperwork, these must be Chet Isley and Darren Babineaux, dragged into the principal's office for fighting. Ten years down the road, would Sam or Tyler be in similar circumstances? *I'll be raising teenagers.* Heaven help him.

A moment later, a girl biked into the lot, joining them after she'd securely chained her bicycle. She was nearly as tall as Grayson, her head shaved on one side, and she had what looked like a tattoo on her forearm, but once she stood next to him, he realized the lines were drawn on with pen and beginning to smudge.

"Mona Flores?" he asked, checking the list. "Here for skipping class."

"Ma-ath," she said, drawing it out to two disdainful syllables. "I'm going to art school, not joining an engineering program. So what if I ditched one period?"

"One?" The burlier of the two boys snorted. "Half your teachers couldn't pick you out of a lineup."

She leveled a glare at him. "Funny you should mention lineups, Isley. Heard your brother was arrested again. You keep starting fights, the two of you can share a cell. It'll be like a family reunion!"

The kid with the goatee—Babineaux, by default—laughed, and Isley shoved his shoulder. Grayson promptly inserted himself between them before hostilities could escalate. "Knock it off. If the three of you don't learn from your mistakes, you'll be spending a lot more weekends together—and that's a best-case scenario." He handed Mona a pair of gloves and a bag. "Getting expelled could hurt your chances of getting into art school. Stick with your classes. *All* of them."

As she tugged on the gloves, he added, "When I was in school, I hated physics. It's not like I was going to be a scientist and Mr. Sherman was the most boring man alive."

Babineaux groaned. "Sherman is the *worst*."

"Well, when I started doing professional rodeo, I discovered that force and acceleration are part of successful bull riding. Learn everything you can while you're in school, you never know what you might need later. Mona, if you're no good at calculating time spent and supply costs, how will you know what to charge people for your brilliant artwork?"

Her lips twitched. "Yeah, yeah, yeah." Equipment in hand, she headed down the sidewalk.

He turned to the other two. "As for you—"

Isley rolled his eyes. "Is this where you tell us we should put aside our differences and become buddies?"

"Do I look like an idiot to you? *Don't*," he added when Babineaux opened his mouth to respond. "What I was going to say was, it's a big park. Plenty of room for you to split up and focus on collecting litter instead of antagonizing each other. Frankly, I don't care if the two of you get along or not." At seventeen, nothing in the world could have coerced him to befriend Reggie George. Hell, he wasn't sure he could bring himself to buddy up to the man *now*.

But maybe he owed the man an apology for that stunt with the high-school mascot. Previous years of Reggie being awful did not excuse the awful thing Grayson had done. Would the man be attending the reunion tonight?

The only person he knew for sure was going was Hadley. *If you change your mind, come say hi.* When she'd issued that invitation, only days ago, she'd still liked him. The thought that he might've lost her friendship ate away at him like an acid burn. If he went to the reunion, he could apologize in person. She might see that he was trying to face his past, trying to do better.

Or she might throw a cup of punch in his face. Only one way to find out.

Chapter Eight

The high-school gymnasium had never looked more festive. Alumni entered through a balloon arch in the school colors, and everything inside was decorated with tiny twinkle lights. Hadley, who'd treated herself to a new dress from the local boutique, felt appropriately elegant. But hardly festive.

"Hadley the Cannon!"

Managing not to wince at the moniker, she turned toward a cluster of women she'd played softball with—Heather, Maisie, Lorina and Pris. The latter two still lived in the county, but Hadley hadn't seen the others since the day they'd signed her cast after senior year. There were hugs all around—although they had to hug Lorina from the side because she was heavily pregnant.

Maisie, who'd traveled from Arizona to be at the reunion, eyed the baby bump. "You aren't going to deliver here, are you? Did any of our graduating class go into obstetrics?"

Lorina laughed. "I look about fifteen months pregnant, don't I? But he's not due for another six weeks."

She turned to Hadley. "You and I haven't seen much of each other since I moved to Turtle, but I'd love for you to come to the baby shower."

Hadley nodded. "Email me the date and time, and I'll see what I can do."

"I haven't seen much of any of you," Maisie said, pouting. "I have friends in Arizona, but I miss my girls! Are Angel and Brighton coming tonight?"

"Angel, yes," Lorina said. Her expression turned somber. "But Brighton just lost her mom."

A hush fell over the group, and Hadley felt a rush of sympathy for her friend. She shivered as she thought about her own mother. How different would life be if Wanda hadn't survived that stroke? It was too horrible to contemplate. The EMTs told Hadley that her 911 call had helped save her mother's life. After a stroke that massive, immediate emergency care was critical. *What if I hadn't been with her?* Hadley's dad had been on a fishing trip, and Leanne had been living out of state at the time. If she'd moved away to college as planned, started a new life outside of Cupid's Bow...

Conversation slowly turned to lighter topics, from jobs to long-ago antics on the team bus. Lorina's husband approached to ask if she wanted to get off her feet for a bit, and they began scouting for a table with empty seats.

Heather was looking around when she stopped and let out a low whistle. "*He* must be one of the significant others in attendance because I feel like I'd remember if he'd gone to school with us."

Hadley followed her friend's gaze and did a double

take at the sight of Grayson in a pair of black jeans, a white button-down shirt and a black suit jacket that emphasized his broad shoulders. "Grayson," she breathed.

"You know him?" Maisie asked. "I guess that's a stupid question, since he's coming right for you."

It was true. His eyes had locked on her, and while he wasn't exactly rushing through the crowd, his stride was purposeful as he made his way toward her. She couldn't read his expression from this far away, but her heart fluttered. Had he come tonight because of her? Was he here to apologize again? He could have done that by phone without getting dressed up.

Although, those jeans and that jacket could be considered a strategic move. It would be difficult for a woman to push him away looking like that.

Did she *want* to push him away? She was still angry, but she didn't hate him. He'd had a tough childhood and he'd made some horrible decisions.

But he hadn't let it define his whole life. He was a responsible adult now, not a surly teen. She'd seen how fantastic he was with those boys, and he didn't have to go around town changing lightbulbs and gifting bird feeders. That was his conscience at work, his willingness to atone. If he could put aside a troubled past, was he worth another chance?

Make up your mind quick. Because he'd reached her.

"Hadley. You look beautiful," he said hoarsely.

She was too emotionally conflicted to know how to reply. "Grayson, these are some of my softball buddies. Heather, Maisie, Lorina, Pris. You guys remember Grayson Cox?"

He smiled at her friends. "Would you ladies mind if I steal Hadley for a few minutes?"

Heather leaned forward and whispered loudly, "Hadley, go dance with him before I do."

From the surprised expression on Grayson's face, Hadley knew he hadn't come over here to ask her to dance. He'd probably intended for them to talk in some secluded corner. But maybe it was time to actually participate instead of isolating himself on the sidelines like he had when they were in high school.

"Let's dance," she told him, a note of challenge in her voice.

His eyes widened fractionally, but he nodded.

It wasn't until they'd almost reached the dance floor that she realized how slow the song was and regretted her bravado. But then his arms slid around her, pulling her close, distracting her from second thoughts.

"I can't believe you're here," she said.

"I need to find Reggie George and apologize."

She was so startled she almost tripped over his feet. It was absolutely the last thing she'd expected him to say. "But you can't stand Reggie."

"I can't stand myself. I can't stand what I did. Or that I hurt you." His hold on her tightened protectively, as if he was trying to stop her from falling ten years too late. "I'm sorry that I can't change who I was a decade ago, but I can do my damnedest to be better. Apologizing to Reggie is part of that."

He was going to take the high road with a guy

who'd allegedly tormented him for years? *Because he's a good man.* The shell of anger around her heart cracked a little.

"I'm also here because I need to talk to you," he admitted. His eyes were pools of emotion; she couldn't remember the last time anyone had looked at her so intently. "But, to tell you the truth, I still haven't figured out what to say."

"Maybe I can help. I did a lot of thinking last night." And all day today. Given how preoccupied she'd been while shelving books, the next few weeks at the library would be like a wacky scavenger hunt. "Neither of us will ever know where I'd be right now if I hadn't lost my scholarship."

He flinched.

"But I know where I am now, and I like it here. I love my job, and I'm imminently grateful I was with my mother when she had her stroke. With a severe brain-stem stroke, every minute counts. If she'd been alone and unable to call 911…" Her voice broke, and he cradled her closer, offering warmth and silent support. It felt indescribably good, so she leaned into him.

"I know you never intended to hurt me. What you did was lousy, but…" She craned her head, meeting his eyes. "I forgive you." She brushed a quick kiss across his cheek.

When he sucked in a breath, she felt suddenly shy.

"I, ah, hope that wasn't out of line," she murmured.

"Are you kidding? Hitting me with your car would have been out of line. But understandable. What you just gave me was an incredible gift." He slid his thumb over her bottom lip.

How could just the pad of his finger elicit so much sensation?

"I'll try to be worthy of it," he promised.

"I know you will. And I can help you on your quest! I'll be like your sidekick." She said it lightly, but he didn't return her smile.

"*Quest* is a heroic term." He looked away. "I feel more like a coward than a hero. Do you think if I flat-out told people about the things I did that it would hurt Violet's standing in the community? Or that it could affect the boys?"

She was quiet, considering her neighbors. Some of them held grudges. "It's hard to predict how people would react, and apologies aren't tangible. I think you're on the right track with the lightbulbs and bird feeders. They may be small acts of atonement, but they're actual, palpable ways of improving someone's day. And I know the community better than you do. I can point you in the direction of people who could use a boost."

"Like Ashley, the little girl who wants to go to Space Camp."

"And Sandra Feller."

He cocked his head, as if trying to place the name. "Didn't the kids call her Sandra Flower when we were growing up?"

"She was the longest running president of the Cupid's Bow Gardening Society, but she stepped down when she started chemo. She's finished with treatment now, but her yard's more barren than it's ever looked. Maybe we could plant a rosebush or something. Mr. Weber used to drive to the tiny German bakery in Hotzler once a month to get *lebkuchen* spice cookies like his mother used to make. He's getting too old to make the trip, but the bakery doesn't ship. And someone should do something nice for Mr. Garcia."

"Ned Garcia?" At her nod, he asked gingerly, "Is there…is he sick or something?"

"No, but he must be so lonely. His business partner and his wife are both dead now. His only son joined the army and was killed in the Middle East. Ned is such a nice man."

"That's what Vi said, too." A moment later, he added, "And she may be a better judge of character than you."

She heaved a sigh. "Because I dated Reggie?" She thought he'd moved past this.

"No, because you think *I'm* an okay guy."

"You're more than *okay*."

"See?" He grinned, his dimples making her heart do a little somersault. "You're a terrible judge of character."

GRAYSON STOOD NEXT to Hadley while she discussed careers with some of her former teammates. For the most part, he was counting his blessings. Hadley's forgiveness made him feel like the luckiest man in the building. But he couldn't help squirming when one of the women, now a flight attendant, began sharing her travel anecdotes. When Hadley was younger, she'd wanted to see the world. Yet here she was, two decades later, still in Cupid's Bow. How did she not hate him?

And why, when people asked about what she'd been up to, didn't she mention the stories she'd had published or the residency she'd applied for? He was surprised. Even in the short time he'd been back, he realized how important her writing was to her. Didn't she want to share that with her friends?

"Hey." She nudged him gently, her voice a whisper as Lorina listed the baby names she and her husband had brainstormed. "Do you still want to apologize to Reggie?"

Want was a strong word. This was going to be more unpleasant than being stepped on by a bull. "You see him?"

She pointed. The ex-football player stood by the stage with a statuesque redhead two inches taller than him.

Grayson ground his teeth. "Might as well get this over with."

They drifted in Reggie's direction, stopping along the way as Hadley greeted various acquaintances. By the time they finally reached her ex-boyfriend, the man had spotted Hadley. He smiled at her, but then stared in confusion at Grayson.

"Cox? Is that you?" He flashed Hadley a toothy grin. "Damn, sweetheart, I guess your standards really slipped after me. Kidding! How the hell are you guys? Hadley, Grayson, this is my wife, Mrs. Juliette George." He patted the woman's stomach. "You can't tell yet because her body's so banging, but we're expecting baby number two."

"Congratulations," Hadley told the redhead.

Meanwhile, Grayson wondered how Reggie ever got *either* of these women to give him the time of day. "We won't keep you," Grayson said. "I'm sure you want to catch up with all of your old buddies. But while we're all here tonight, I have a confession to make. Do you remember that stolen donkey mascot from—"

"That was you!" Reggie's face became mottled with rage. For half a second, Grayson thought the man might actually take a swing at him.

He was entitled. After all, there had been a time when Reggie had deep feelings for Hadley. He'd witnessed firsthand how much Grayson's thoughtless stunt had hurt her.

"My father almost didn't believe me when I said I wasn't behind that," Reggie said. "He threatened to take back the convertible I got for graduation!"

Grayson gaped at the man. "*That's* what you're mad about?"

"Honey, your blood pressure," Juliette cautioned her husband.

Reggie took several deep breaths, then socked Grayson in the arm. "I guess it all worked out okay. Got to keep the car, and it made me look like a badass to all the students who thought I really was responsible. I appreciate you coming clean, but no harm done, man."

No harm? Grayson's temper rose, but he wasn't sure which of them he was mad at. "No harm except for Hadley's broken arm, torn shoulder ligament and lost scholarship. Her whole future..."

"Oh. Well. Yeah." Reggie shifted uncomfortably. "But you're good now, right, Hadley? Work at a bookstore?"

"The library, actually."

Reggie gave her a fond smile, then told his wife, "Hadley and I first hooked up in the library. She needed my help with a school project." At Hadley's glare, he amended, "Well, maybe it was more like mutual assistance. Hey, Andersen!" he suddenly hollered at a guy crossing the room. "Come on, Juliette, I've gotta show you off to the team quarterback. Grayson, Hadley, you kids have fun tonight. Don't do anything I wouldn't do."

Momentarily speechless, Grayson and Hadley watched them fade into the crowd.

"Huh." She turned to Grayson, her expression deadpan. "I don't know if you've ever noticed before, but... that man is kind of an ass."

The outrage he'd been feeling on her behalf evaporated into amusement. He threw his head back and laughed. It was too loud, drawing quizzical stares from others, but it was cleansing. He felt lighter than he had in weeks. "You want to go outside for some fresh air?"

"Yes, please."

There was a door that led out the side of the gym. He opened it for her, the spring night cool around them. They weren't the only ones who'd escaped the crowd inside. Couples sat on the hoods of cars in the parking lot and small clusters of people chatting dotted the campus. But there was no one within earshot when he shrugged out of his jacket and spread it over the grass for her like a picnic blanket.

"Thank you." She kicked off her shoes and sat with her knees bent to the side, trying to move over enough so that there was room for him on the fabric.

He laughed. "I appreciate the thought, but you're the one in the dress. I promise my jeans have seen worse than the school lawn." But no sooner had the words left his mouth than he realized he'd cheated himself out of a golden opportunity, seizing an excuse to scoot as close to her as possible. Holding her on the dance floor had left him craving more of her.

The smart move was for them to remain platonic friends, but after thinking about her all day, worrying that he'd lost her, he couldn't deny that he wanted more. What did Hadley want?

"Is it selfish that I brought you out here?" he asked. "I don't want to keep you from your friends."

"I'll go back in soon." She turned, meeting his eyes. "Right now, this is right where I want to be."

Me, too. There were things he wanted to say, but somehow, they seemed both inadequate and too much all at once. He looked up, trying to see the stars, but the lights in the parking lot obscured all but the brightest of them. "Your friends are nice."

"The best," she agreed. "I hope I do a better job of keeping up with them between now and the twentieth reunion."

He smiled at her. "Maybe you'll be a best-selling novelist by then. Why didn't you mention to them that you write?" Or had she told them all about it before he showed up tonight?

"I… It's not exactly as secret, but it isn't easy for me to talk about, either. There's a high level of anxiety. Writing is so different from softball. On the field, you know instantly if you're doing a good job. Results are immediate—you get the base or the run, or you get tagged out. The crowd reacts. Writing is lonely. It's just you and the blank page and the blinking cursor of doom."

He chuckled at that.

"It can take days, weeks, to finish even short pieces, then you send them out into the world and wait for the referee to make some kind of call. Even if it's published, you'll never know how most readers respond to it."

"You make it sound nerve-racking."

"It is. But thrilling, too." She wiggled her bare toes out in front of her. "I wonder if this is how painters feel. You put something on the canvas in the solitude of your studio, unsure whether people will declare it a work of abstract genius or just stare at it and mutter 'I don't get it.' And some artists are only celebrated later, not appreciated during their own time."

"Granted I'm new at it, but I think parenting is like that, too. You put in the effort every day, but it's difficult to know whether you're doing a good job until way down the road, when you can see the kind of person a kid has become. And even then, it's not really an end result. Adults continue to grow and change."

"Hopefully. Some of us probably stagnate, afraid to challenge ourselves to leave our comfort zones."

Did she feel like she was stagnating here in Cupid's Bow? He bumped his shoulder against hers. "Is Colorado in your comfort zone?"

She laughed. "Hardly. I've never been that far from home. And I'd be gone six months! Inconvenient timing, considering Sierra's wedding, but she's been totally supportive. She told me not to worry about logistics until I actually get the residency—and not to worry about it then because I should be too busy celebrating."

"I only met her briefly, but she seems terrific. Very..."

"Lively? Outspoken? Feisty?"

He grinned. "Something like that. Jarrett is clearly crazy about her. I'm going to the ranch tomorrow afternoon so he can introduce me to the students I'll be working with and smooth the transition. He even invited me to bring the boys to come see the animals and run around in the wide-open spaces."

"Maybe I'll see you there. Sierra's bridesmaids are meeting to get her input on the bridal shower and do a preliminary dress fitting. Sierra's parents are throwing a lot of money into 'Cupid's Bow's wedding of the century,' but the Ross family wanted to contribute, as well. Jarrett's mom is sewing the bridesmaid dresses. In fact, if the timing works out, maybe we can ride together to the ranch."

Seeing her again so soon? "I'd like that. For now, though, I should actually get going. I agreed to help the construction foreman move in the morning." It was both a good deed *and* sucking up to the boss in the name of job security. "Can I walk you back inside?"

She nodded, leaning over to rest her head against his shoulder. "I'm so glad you were here. I wasn't in a great mood when I left the house, but tonight turned out to be nearly perfect."

"Nearly?"

Her gaze dropped to his mouth, and the need to kiss her was overwhelming. He wasn't entirely sure it was a good idea—but he was damn sure it was what they both wanted. He tipped her chin up with his finger, searching her expression for permission.

Her lips parted around a sigh, and he leaned in to temptation. She tasted sweet, her mouth hot and welcoming. Back when they'd gone to school here, he'd never participated in proms or pep rallies or homecoming. But Hadley's kiss was its own kind of homecoming. She threaded her fingers through his hair, clutching him closer, and he was exactly where he was supposed to be in the world.

It wasn't until some reunion-goers passed by too closely that he remembered where they were. He pulled away while he still could, resisting the impulse to lie her against his discarded jacket and trace more kisses along the curve of her ear, the hollow of her throat, the tantalizing dip of her cleavage.

"Wow," she breathed.

"Tell me about it." He rested his forehead against hers. "If you write half as well as you kiss, you'd better start packing for Colorado."

It was a strangely reassuring notion, that she might be headed west soon. Because, if she stayed here, it would be damn difficult to keep from falling for her.

THE DAY THEY'D had lunch together, Grayson had mentioned he'd arrived back in Cupid's Bow at night, and now Hadley understood why he'd chosen to make the trip while the twins were asleep. They never shut up. The drive to the Twisted R had never been more interminable.

Every time one of the boys started to tell her something, the other interrupted with something to add. Sam told her all about the Big Dipper and Little Dipper while Tyler wanted to talk about the garden and how spinach didn't taste as bad as he'd feared, but that it didn't make your muscles bulge out like in the cartoons. From there, the conversation spun to favorite animated shows and movies, with Tyler outing Sam for having a nightmare about a movie that "wasn't even scary." Grayson reprimanded Tyler, pointing out that people feared different things, and a discussion of phobias followed.

Sam leaned forward as far as his seat belt would allow, trying to poke his head in the front seat with the adults. "What are you afraid of, Miss Hadley?"

"Never having another moment's peace and quiet?" Grayson asked under his breath.

Hadley laughed.

"What? What's funny?" Tyler demanded. "Gray, did you make a silly face?"

"My silly faces are the hit of bedtime," he boasted.

"And he makes silly noises, too," Sam added. "He can—"

"Oh, I don't think Miss Hadley needs to hear about all that," Grayson said firmly. "In fact, maybe we should play the quiet game for a few minutes."

"Sounds boring," Tyler said suspiciously.

"But it might be good practice for school," Grayson said. "You guys know you need to be quiet when the teacher is talking, right? And when the class is working on something, it's best to only talk if you have a question. And then you raise your hand."

"We know." Sam's voice held a hint of exasperation, and Hadley suspected this wasn't the first time the boys had heard the back-to-school lecture.

"You two will get to meet Alyssa and Mandy at the ranch," she said. Her friend Kate was one of the other bridesmaids and would have her stepdaughters with her. "They're a couple of years older than you, but they go to Cupid's Bow Elementary, too. You can ask them about kindergarten if you have questions. And guess what? They're identical twins, like you."

"Cool! We knew some twins in Oklahoma, but they were practically babies," Sam said. "Too little to play with. Maybe Alyssa and Mandy can be our friends."

"They're girls," Tyler pointed out.

His brother shrugged. "Girls aren't bad."

"Girls are awesome." Grayson turned to look at the boys. "Just think about Violet and Hadley."

"And our mom?" Sam asked softly.

From Grayson's surprised expression, Hadley got the impression the twins didn't mention their late parents often. Did he ever broach the subject, keeping the boys' parents alive in their memory, or was it hard for him to talk about his friends?

"Yeah, buddy, your mom was the best," Grayson said, his voice thick, "and she loved you and your brother very much."

Silence fell then, and Hadley wondered what it must be like for the boys to relocate to a place where no one had known their parents. "Do you have pictures of your mom at Violet's house?" she asked tentatively. "Maybe you could show them to me sometime. If you want."

"And Daddy, too?" Tyler asked eagerly.

"Absolutely. They must have been pretty special people to have kids like you and a friend like Grayson."

The boys nodded happily, and Grayson reached across the seat to squeeze her hand, a gesture she took as silent gratitude. Simple appreciation—no reason for her stomach to somersault and her skin to feel flushed. Except that ever since that kiss last night, Hadley felt different around him. Responded to him differently.

She shouldn't read too much in to it. They'd been in a romantic surrounding, enjoying a nostalgic evening that brought them closer. A kiss good-night was a natural conclusion. It didn't cancel out Grayson's earlier statements that he had his hands full with the boys and wasn't ready for romance.

Yet.

Was she projecting the word onto him? Maybe she shouldn't, but just because he felt overwhelmed right now didn't mean he would forever. Writers often had to be patient. It had taken her weeks to write the first short story she submitted and she'd waited *months* to hear back from the magazine.

Grayson was a man who would be worth the wait.

Chapter Nine

"Why are all of you so tall?" Sierra Bailey grumbled. She was definitely the shortest of the five women in the living room. But, then, she was often the shortest adult in any room. "Everyone is going to tower over me in the wedding pictures."

"That may be the first time I've ever been described as tall," Mrs. Ross said around the pin in her mouth. She'd just finished Becca Johnston's fitting and had moved on to Kate Trent's dress.

Hadley sat on the couch in her regular clothes, waiting her turn and occasionally checking the kitchen, where both sets of twins were playing a board game. The only bridesmaid not here today was the groom's sister, Vicki, who was away at college, but Mrs. Ross had her daughter's measurements.

"I can't believe how fast you're losing the baby weight," Mrs. Ross said, adjusting the waist of Kate's unfinished dress.

"*I* can't believe she didn't bring the baby with her so we could coo over how cute she is," Becca complained.

Kate shot the mayor an apologetic look. "Cole feels

like he doesn't get much one-on-one bonding time with her. Since Luke's running a 5K with friends and I have the twins with me, today was a perfect opportunity."

"Speaking of running," Becca said, "I'd better get changed and get out of here. Sorry I can't stay longer."

"Town emergency?" Hadley asked.

"No, Marc has a soccer game. I promised I'd be there before it's over."

"Well, at least you got to stay long enough to meet Hadley's cowboy," Sierra declared. "Dreamy!"

"He is supercute," Kate said, obligingly raising her arms so Mrs. Ross could keep pinning.

Hadley could object that Gray wasn't "her" cowboy, but she couldn't protest that he wasn't good-looking. He was wildly attractive, and not just because of his build, or his thick hair or those mesmerizing dark eyes. There was—

"Hadley?" Sierra's voice was a loud whisper, meant to carry. "Your cheeks are going all rosy. Something you'd like to share with the rest of the class?"

Hadley glared at her friend. "I'm going to get a glass of water. Which I may or may not dump on you."

The other women chuckled, but they didn't drop the subject. After Hadley returned with ice water and Becca had hugged everyone goodbye, Kate asked, "So how long have you known Grayson?"

"We both grew up here," Hadley said, "so, forever. I mean, I don't remember specifically meeting him. He was just there, in my classes, on the playground, at the high school. And now he's back."

"Romantic," Kate sighed. "It's like life is giving you a second chance."

"More like a first one. We weren't close before. And I'm not saying we are now!" she added before Sierra could make any knowing comments. "We're still getting to know each other." For instance, just last night, she'd discovered what a skilled kisser he was.

"Well, watch out," Sierra said, "it can happen fast. After all, I only worked for the Ross family for a couple of weeks and now—"

"And now she *is* family," her future mother-in-law said, eyes misty. She sniffled, turning back to Kate. "All done, dear. You go change while I get a tissue. Hadley, you're up."

"The dress is hanging in Vicki's room," Sierra said. "I'll show you."

This wasn't Hadley's first time on the ranch, but normally she visited the refurbished cottage Jarrett and Sierra shared, about twenty acres from the main house.

Sierra led her down the hall, and Hadley smiled at the royal blue dress. Mrs. Ross had used the same fabric for all four bridesmaids, but each had her own design. "It's even prettier than the picture we saw."

"You're all going to look gorgeous. I can't wait for the big day!"

"Really? I hadn't noticed how the wedding comes up in every conversation. Or, how when Jarrett walks into the room, you forget anyone else exists," she teased.

Sierra brandished one of the throw pillows from the bed at her. "Hey, don't make me sound pathetic."

"Not pathetic. Just happy. You two are perfect for each other."

"Maybe that's why I've been encouraging you to spend more time with Grayson," Sierra said. "I want you to be as happy as me and Kate and Becca. Not that a woman needs a man to be happy, but you're different around him. When the two of you got out of the car, you looked almost giddy."

"Because the ride was over and I was no longer trapped in a closed space with Sam and Tyler. They talked my ears off."

Sierra tilted her head, expression thoughtful. "I guess it could be complicated to fall for someone who has kids. Kate and Cole made it work, but she was already an experienced mom. Would it be weird for you, becoming a stepmother?"

"Stepmother! The man's only kissed me once, and you—"

"*Whoa.* Hold the phone. The two of you kissed?"

"Last night. At the reunion." She sank down onto the bed. "It was heavenly."

Her friend pumped a fist in the air. "Yes!"

"But it was a one-time thing." Possibly.

Sierra winked. "Everything is a one-time thing… until it happens a second time."

SOMEHOW, SIERRA TALKED Hadley and Grayson in to bringing the boys up to the cottage and staying for dinner. It was difficult for Hadley to be annoyed at her friend's pushiness when dinner was so wonderful—and not just because of the food. She was entranced watching Grayson joke with the twins and reminisce with Jarrett about rodeo life. *I've never seen him this relaxed.* His dimples were in full force tonight—and when he smiled in her direction, a tingle went all the way through her straight down to her toes.

She was enjoying one of those tingles when she caught Sierra smirking at her. *Oops.* Cutting into the expertly grilled steak, Hadley tried to think of something besides Grayson's dimples. "So, uh, how are the wedding plans going? Did you settle on the invitations yet?" The couple had sent out their save the date cards weeks ago, but were still trying to agree on the final invitations.

"There are plenty we like," Sierra said unenthusiastically, "but none that strike me as *perfect* yet."

Jarrett put his arm around her. "All I need for *perfect* is you and me hitched at the end of the day, darlin'."

"They just seem too generic. 'Fill in the blank' and 'fill in the blank' request your presence at their wedding at blank o'clock."

Tyler glanced up from his plate in confusion; both boys were chowing down following an active afternoon of play. "What's blank o'clock?"

"She didn't mean it literally," Grayson said.

"Oh." Tyler paused. "What's *literally*?"

While Grayson tried to sort that out with the boys, Hadley said, "What you need is something to personalize it. A lyric from a song you've danced to, or a quote from a favorite movie."

"Yeah, that works for *you*," Sierra said, "you have

a romantic streak. But Jarrett's favorite movie is *Die Hard*. We are *not* putting 'yippee-ki-yay' on the invites."

Hadley giggled. "It would be memorable."

"And just think how much your parents would hate it," Jarrett told his fiancée.

"Hmm. I do enjoy irritating them. Still." Sierra shook her head. "It's not exactly what I want to look back on during our golden years."

"Maybe a line of poetry would be more elegant?" Hadley suggested.

Grayson looked toward her, a mischievous twinkle in his eye. "Hadley was showing me a book of poems at the library the other day. Maybe she could recommend a selection from it."

Her cheeks warmed as she thought about the erotic verses, and his grin widened.

"Or maybe you could write us something," Sierra said.

"What?" Hadley's attention snapped back to her friend. "Oh, I don't think so! Poems aren't my specialty."

"You're too modest about your talent." Sierra turned to Grayson. "Can you believe I had to buy a magazine to finally read her stuff? Heaven knows how she applied for that residency when she's so neurotic about showing her work to anyone."

"That's different," Hadley protested. "Sending pages to total strangers in a different state isn't as nerve-racking as showing my stories to my very opinionated friends. It's not like we can avoid each other if you hate my work, and I don't want people to feel like they have to pretend. Besides, I needed the practice mailing off my stories. Someday, I hope to be able to submit something without getting nauseous."

"What's nauseous?" Tyler asked.

"I know!" his brother said excitedly. "It's like when you're about to yarf."

"Oh." Tyler leaned forward to see past Grayson's broad shoulders. "I hope you don't yarf, Miss Hadley."

She bit back a laugh. "Thanks." Aware that there'd been a lot of dinner conversation that excluded the boys, she asked them if the girls had told them lots of good things about living in Cupid's Bow.

"To tell you the truth," Sierra said conspiratorially, "*I* didn't like Cupid's Bow when I first moved here. It's hard to get delivery food, and it's easy to get lost and the theater never seems to show the movies I want to see. But have you tried the ice-cream parlor on Main Street? It's incredible. And the stars here are amazing at night."

That got Sam's attention. "Vi's teaching me about constellations! One day I wanna see them through a microscope and—"

"It's telescope," Tyler said with an exaggerated eye roll. "Like telephone."

Sam scowled. "I don't wanna talk to the stars, I just wanna see 'em."

"We have a telescope," Sierra said. "Jarrett bought it for my birthday. The stars are the best part of living on the ranch."

"A-*hem.*" Jarrett raised his eyebrows, and she laughed, leaning over to kiss him.

"Second best part," she amended. "You boys want to take a look after dessert?"

"I wish we could stay that long," Grayson said, "but the boys start school in the morning. I really need to get these buckaroos home to bed."

This was met with groans and complaints, but obviously the boys were more tired than they wanted to admit because they were uncharacteristically quiet on the drive back to Violet's.

As Grayson removed their booster seats from the back of Hadley's car, Sam walked up to the driver-side window, his eyes wide and imploring. "Will you come in and read a story with us?"

The invitation tugged at her heart, but Grayson had already told them they needed to make a beeline for the bathtub. "Maybe another time. But what I can do," she said, compromising, "is come give you a good-night hug." She climbed out of the car, sweeping both boys into her arms. "You two be good at school tomorrow, okay?"

After the boys dutifully nodded and turned toward the house, Grayson instructed, "Tell Aunt Vi I'll be there in just a minute." Once they were inside, he took Hadley's hand, tugging her around the corner and out of view.

She batted her eyelashes at him. "Did you want a good-night hug, too?"

His wicked smile sent a tremor of anticipation through her. "I have a better idea." And then he was kissing her.

He traced her lips with his tongue and her pulse kicked up a notch as he deepened the kiss. The tremor she'd experienced was replaced with a more pleasurable quiver deep and low. She gripped his shoulders, lost in the longing that had surged to life.

When he finally, reluctantly, pulled away, they were both breathing hard.

"I'd better go inside before someone comes looking for me," he said. But he didn't move toward the door.

She ran her hands over his back, reveling in the muscles beneath her fingers. "I'm starting to think you like me."

The corner of his mouth kicked up in a sexy half grin. "Maybe you and I can get together tomorrow night without the boys and discuss just how much."

"If only. Leanne has a major literature project due this week and I promised my assistance. We could be working pretty late. I'd have to check my calendar to be sure, but Tuesday might work."

"Not for me," he said regretfully. "I have this thing I promised Vi I'd do. Trust me, I'd rather be with you."

"Wednesday night is wide open. Hint, hint."

He grinned. "Then it's a date."

I have a date with Grayson. Since she was a grown woman, she managed not to squeal with delight—until she was alone in her car. Wednesday couldn't get here soon enough.

VI HAD THE boys in the tub by the time Grayson entered the house, so he headed to the kitchen for a cold glass of water. *As if that will be enough to cool you down.*

After Hadley's kisses, he could jump into an arctic lake and still have heat surging through his veins. He mentally replayed their brief but passionate embrace. The way she—

"Well, you look pretty pleased with yourself," Vi commented from the doorway. "Your day went well?"

"Very. Oh, hey…any chance you can watch the boys for me for a few hours Wednesday night?" If not, he needed to make other arrangements.

"Sure."

"And how did your day go?" he asked quickly, before she inquired about his plans. When he'd left for the ranch, Violet had been frantically cleaning. Not that her house was ever truly messy, but she'd seemed to have an excess of nervous energy. She was visibly calmer now. "The meeting with Jim was okay?" He'd encouraged her to take her ex as a client before he'd had the whole story. He hoped it hadn't been too uncomfortable for her.

She nodded. "I've always loved the furniture he makes—I still have all three pieces he gave me—and it's gratifying that he gets to do it full-time now. And we talked. About his divorce. About you being back. About life in general. It's pointless to wonder 'what if,' but if things had been different…" Her smile was wistful. "I'd better check on the boys and make sure some of the water is still in the tub."

"I'll do that. Thanks for getting them started."

"While you said goodbye to Hadley?" she asked knowingly. "What are the two of you planning to do Wednesday?"

"We, ah, haven't decided yet."

He'd been hoping that after their time at the ranch, the boys would fall asleep easily. But bath time seemed to have renewed their energy. Or maybe they were nervous about school tomorrow. *He* certainly was. The kids he'd gone to kindergarten with were the same people he graduated with; early impressions mattered. So far, the twins had taken relocating to Cupid's Bow well, but that was easy within the confines of Vi's cozy home. School, where they would be required to interact with other people every day, was the real test.

Even an hour after he tucked them in, they were still finding excuses to call him back.

"Gray?" Sam's voice trailed through the house, easily heard over the baseball game Grayson was watching.

Well, sort of watching. It was on the television while he paced circles in the living room.

"I'll go," Vi said from behind him. "You're as restless as they are tonight—maybe not the best person to lull them to sleep."

He sighed. "It's ridiculous to be this antsy about a first day of kindergarten, isn't it?" But they would be the new kids, trying to figure out where the classroom was and what the rules were when the rest of the class already had months of practice.

She patted his shoulder. "Concern for your kids' well-being is never ridiculous, but they'll probably feel more confident if you're not radiating low-level panic."

Sam called out again, and Vi disappeared down the hallway. Grayson jabbed the remote toward the TV, and the ball game winked into blackness. He needed a better distraction.

He could definitely think of a more pleasant one. In his room, he closed the door and pulled out his phone. He was already scrolling through his contacts for Hadley's number when he stopped himself. He'd spent most of the evening with her. Was he really so needy that he'd call her only a couple of hours after saying goodbye? Pitiful.

He'd reached for the phone without hesitation, the way he used to with Blaine, knowing he could contact his best friend at any time with good news to celebrate or concerns he needed to vent. Hadn't Grayson learned his lesson? Best not to be too dependent on other people. He liked Hadley, but he could wait until Wednesday before he talked to her again.

He needed to wait, for his own peace of mind.

Meanwhile, he needed to channel his energy.

"Where are you off to?" Vi asked when he emerged with his truck keys.

"To do some illicit gardening." Hadley had given him Mrs. Feller's address. He had gardening supplies and two rosebushes in the truck, but he'd wanted to wait until it was late enough that no neighbors would be walking their dogs one last time or watching fireflies from their porches.

His aunt sighed, still conflicted about his late-night good deeds. "Happy planting. And don't get caught."

"That's my motto." Or it had been, once upon a time. But he was a different person now, surrounded by new friends and new opportunities. He was grateful for both but still wary. It was when you let your guard down that life was most likely to knock you on your ass.

STANDING IN SOMEONE else's flower bed at eleven o'clock at night was an odd place to have an epiphany. But it had occurred to Grayson last night outside Mrs. Feller's house that for all the strangers and acquaintances he was trying to help, he'd overlooked the person closest to him. Wasn't it time he repay some small measure of Violet's kindness? So he'd called Jim McKay first thing Monday morning to ask if they could meet for lunch.

"Sorry I'm so grubby," Grayson said as he strolled up to the picnic table, a bag in one hand and a mini-cooler in the other. They'd agreed to meet at the park since it was close to the construction site. "I barely had time to stand in line at the deli before my lunch hour ends. Showering and changing were out of the question."

"No problem," Jim said. "I spend a lot of hours in my shop and am covered in head-to-toe sawdust more often than not. Besides, you offered me a free lunch. I'm not going to nitpick the circumstances." As he accepted the wrapped sandwich Grayson handed over, he added, "Have to say, I was surprised to hear from you, though."

"Because last time you saw me I was a young punk more likely to slam a door in someone's face than share a cordial meal with him?"

"Something like that." He studied Grayson. "Your aunt know you called me?"

"Hell, no. She'd see it as interfering in her life and kick my ass."

Jim chuckled, but shook his head. "We both know the worst thing she would ever do to you is withhold baked goods for a day or two."

Easy for you to say, pal. You're not the one who has a Watermelon Festival meeting to attend tomorrow night. He still couldn't believe Vi had talked him in to that. "Regardless, I didn't tell Vi because this isn't just about her. I have something I need to say." He popped open his can of soda. Did carbonated caffeine count as liquid courage? It wasn't easy to look another man in the eye and admit his shortcomings. "I wanted to apologize for being a crappy teenager, for breaking rules and shoplifting and sneering at everyone else in this town."

Jim's eyes widened. "So I was right? The church graffiti—was that you?"

He nodded. "I didn't care then about how my actions would hurt Vi or her reputation if I got busted. I do now. I told her everything. But if my misdeeds are part of why you and Vi ended things—"

"You can't shoulder the blame there, kid. Violet and I… For all that she has a heart the size of Texas, she can still put up some walls. And me? I'm a selfish SOB. I wanted her all to myself." He sighed. "I cared more about you cutting in to our already limited time than about your problems. I should have made an effort."

"No hard feelings." Grayson squinted against the sun. "But Vi is impressed by people going out of their way to help others. So, if you're ever interested in getting on her good side, I think the local animal shelter could use some volunteers. Or that teen mentorship initiative of hers..."

"Noted. It's encouraging that you think I'd have a chance at getting on her good side."

Vi had been more nervous about sitting down with Jim yesterday than Grayson was about the twins' first week of school; people only got that flustered when they cared. And she was far too young and social to be his spinster aunt. "I want her to be happy," he said simply. "Maybe someday you'll be part of that."

"Maybe."

Grayson balled up his empty sandwich bag and stood, executing a perfect shot into the nearby wastebasket. "And it goes without saying that, should you ever hurt Vi, I work on a site where I have access to a backhoe and cement."

Jim gave a bark of laughter. "You turned out all right, kid."

"Thanks. I'm a work in progress."

Chapter Ten

When you put good into the universe, the universe reciprocates. At least, that's how Grayson felt when he entered the community-center meeting room Tuesday evening, because seated in the circle of committee members was his favorite librarian. He'd practiced restraint in not calling her last night to report on the boys' successful first day of school, but now that they were in the same room together, he couldn't deny how happy he was to see her.

A silver-haired woman in a bright pink sweater and yellow pants greeted him at the door. "Ah, you must be Mr. Cox. I'm Joan Denby, this year's committee chair. We're just waiting on one other person, and we'll get started."

All eyes had turned to him as soon as she said "mister," and he found himself on the receiving end of appraising smiles and surprised glances. He was the only guy in the room.

Hadley bounced out of her chair. "Gray! I see you've met Joan. One of the wonderful things about working with her is she always brings peach preserve cookie bars or pear cake." She led him to a table at the back of the room, where coffee and snacks were set up.

Grayson had a new theory about Cupid's Bow. The flurry of activity that went in to their festivals must be a collective exercise program. Thank heavens he was working hard under the Texas sun every day, or he'd already be ten pounds heavier.

"What are you doing here?" Hadley whispered. "You're the last person I expected to see on the Watermelon Festival committee."

"Aunt Vi convinced me. Over my objections." He grinned down at her. "I might have objected less if I'd known you were on the committee, too."

She laughed softly, that musical sound he adored. "Nice to see you, too. I've spent the last two days wanting to kiss you again," she admitted in a husky murmur.

His pulse quickened. "Any chance people won't notice if we sneak out and neck in the hallway?"

"This is Cupid's Bow. If we neck in the hallway, there will be pictures of it on the front page of the *Chronicle* tomorrow."

"I hate this town," he grumbled.

She elbowed him. "Liar."

He thought of the boys' excitement yesterday evening when they'd talked over each other to tell him about the awesome playground and the library that was "almost as good as Miss Hadley's" and their teacher, Ms. Baker, who could do funny voices during story time. "Okay, it's growing on me." For a long time, he'd felt like Cupid's Bow brought out the worst in him. Now he was ready to see what else it had to offer.

It was dark when the festival meeting ended, but not late. Most of the shops and restaurants around the town square were still open.

"Want to grab a bite?" Grayson asked as he and Hadley exited the community center.

Her expression was apologetic. "Leanne and I didn't make as much progress last night as she'd hoped. I promised her I'd come over once the meeting was done. But you and I are still on for tomorrow, right?"

"Absolutely."

As he walked her to her car, he asked, "What would you like to do tomorrow?" It suddenly occurred to him that while he had plenty of experience with women, he didn't have much experience with *dating*. He'd taken plenty of ladies out to a nice dinner and then back to his trailer or, if he was on the road, back to his hotel room. He could just imagine Violet's outraged reaction if he took Hadley into his room and put a sock on the door.

"Grayson?" She was frowning at him. "You okay? I feel like I lost you there for a second."

He was lucky she looked concerned instead of angry. Asking her input and then promptly checking out of the conversation was a jerk move. "Sorry. I just realized that I..." He censored himself, not wanting to paint himself as a guy whose only romantic interactions had been meaningless sex.

She bit her lip. "Having second thoughts?"

Yes. He was officially taking her out on a date in Cupid's Bow. Which meant, everyone would know. People would speculate on their relationship. And when it ended, he'd keep crossing paths with her, potentially for years to come. *No pressure.* "Just trying to think of a fun casual outing." Had he stressed the word *casual* too much? He enjoyed their time together, but this wasn't going anywhere serious. He had the boys, and she had Colorado. Potentially.

"Don't overthink this," she advised. She pulled a quarter out of her pocket. "Heads, we go bowling. Tails, we see a movie."

He chuckled at her decision-making process—silly, but effective.

She flipped the coin in the air and caught it, slapping it down on her opposite wrist. "Ah, bowling it is."

"That's really what you want to do?"

"Dude, fate has spoken. Best not to challenge it."

"Far be it from me to anger fate."

When they got to her car, he leaned down and brushed his lips against hers. Aware of being on a public street, he straightened before the kiss turned heated, but he slid his hand over her cheek, savoring the moment and not wanting to break contact just yet.

"See you tomorrow." Her voice was a touch breathless, but as she slid into the car, she resumed her normal tone. "I hope you aren't a sore loser. I'm pretty good at bowling."

"Only 'pretty good'?" He gave her a look of mock-sympathy.

She started the car with a laugh. "Bring it on, Grayson."

His truck was on the opposite side of the square, and as he made his way back toward it, his father's old store caught his eye. Both Hadley and Violet said that Ned Garcia was a good man, and their opinions carried a lot of weight with Grayson. Before he could talk himself out of it, he cut across the sidewalk to the store and pushed open the glass door. The familiar smells of leather and feed were welcoming, giving him the same sense of ease he'd experienced on the Twisted R.

Ned Garcia himself was behind the counter. "Grayson!" He beamed at him. "I wasn't sure you'd take me up on my offer to drop by."

Neither was I. "Evening, Mr. Garcia. I happened to be in the area and thought I'd stop in." If he'd known he would be coming here, he would have checked with Violet to see if she needed more dog food. He glanced around, trying to see the place through the eyes of a rational adult, not a kid who'd been programmed to believe his future was stolen out from under him.

"Hasn't changed much, has it?" Ned asked.

"Oh, I don't know about that." He idly turned a carousel of riding gloves. "I hear the place is under better ownership than ever."

Ned came out from behind the counter. "Grayson, I love this store. It is like family to me, now that Elia and my boy are gone. But, I vow to you, I did not set out with the intention to take this place from your dad."

"I believe you. He was…not a great father." The truth poured out of him, and it was liberating. "He was erratic and neglectful, drunk more than he was sober. Not terrific qualities for a businessman."

There was a moment of silence as they both remembered Bryant Cox, a deeply flawed man they'd nonetheless cared about.

Grayson cleared his throat. "Vi said you tried to get him to go to meetings, to get help. Thank you for that."

"I'm just sorry I could not do more. But perhaps I can now. I'm pushing seventy, and much as I love the store, it's time to cut back my hours. Spend a lazy morning or two fishing, take the occasional siesta. Any chance you might want a job? You could learn the ropes…maybe take my place one day."

Work at Bryant's store? "I don't know what to say."

"There's not much in the way of staff. Nina Ruiz still puts in a few hours a week, but now that she's got her real-estate license, she has less and less time for the store. And there's a kid from the high school who comes in after class, real responsible sort, but he'll be off to college in August. I could replace him with another teenager, but that's not a long-term solution."

Now that he was a parent, Grayson also needed solid long-term plans. He couldn't see himself working construction for the next twenty years. There was a strong chance the construction foreman would hire him again once the church renovation was complete, but it was good to have other options.

His dad's store, though? The place where Bryant and Rachel had begun their ultimately doomed relationship?

Ned clapped him on the back. "Of course, you'll

need time to consider it, and I'd have to crunch a lot of numbers before I could even—"

"Mr. Garcia, thank you for the offer, but this isn't the place for me." When he thought of the store, he still thought about his father ranting, practically frothing at the mouth. It wasn't a pleasant association.

"Well, that's disappointing but understandable. You know where to find me if you change your mind."

"SO, YOU AND HADLEY..." Vi kept her tone light and her gaze on the spaghetti noodles she was pouring into the strainer, but Grayson squirmed as if under interrogation. "Is this getting serious?"

The word lodged under his skin like a splinter. "How could it be serious? This is our first date."

She turned to him then, her eyebrow cocked. "Not by my count."

"Then you should double-check your math."

"Did you just sass your aunt?"

"No, ma'am." He backpedaled before he found himself not only signed up for another festival committee, but also chairing the damn thing.

"All right then." She reached into a cabinet for plates. "Will you tell the boys to wash up on your way out? Dinner's ready."

He hoped they saved him some; Vi's homemade spaghetti sauce was the best he'd ever had. But he and Hadley planned to grab burgers at the bowling alley. It might not be five-star food, but it would be five-star company.

Whistling softly, he went into the living room,

where the boys were racing cars around a plastic track. He was met with identical glares.

"Miss Hadley is going to be sad," Sam informed him. "Because you're not bringing us with you."

"Yeah," Tyler agreed. "She likes us."

"Yes, she does. She likes you a lot," he assured them as he kneeled down. "But tonight is a dinner for grown-ups."

The boys exchanged glances. "So was dinner with Miss Sierra and Mr. Jarrett," Sam said. "And we were good."

"Very, very good," Tyler insisted. "We'll behave if you take us with you."

"Please." Sam's eyes were huge.

Saying no to that expression made Grayson feel like a monster. He might as well have come into the room growling and stomping on their toy cars. "Tell you what," he began, "tonight I am going out with Miss Hadley by myself. But if you're good for Vi, I'll ask Miss Hadley to come over this weekend and have dinner with us. Deal?"

The twins shared a look. "Will she read us a story?" Sam asked.

Grayson bit back a laugh at the realization that he was negotiating with a five-year-old. "Well, I can't make promises for her, but that seems like a safe bet."

"And can we make ice-cream sundaes when she comes over?" Tyler asked.

Grayson tousled the boy's hair. "Don't push it."

He gave them both hugs, supervised handwashing for dinner and headed to Hadley's house. It was a bit off the beaten path, even for Cupid's Bow, but he'd been familiarizing himself with the roads. Late Monday night, he'd replaced faded and illegible numbers on a woman's mailbox, and before going to work this morning he'd left a cooler of authentic *lebkuchen* cookies at Mr. Weber's front door.

Hadley's home was a small one-story, not much bigger than Sierra and Jarrett's place. The welcome mat said Reader Sanctuary and there was a sign by the front door that said No Soliciting… Unless You're Selling Books. Grinning, he rang the doorbell.

"Just a minute!" When she answered the door a few moments later, she was wearing jeans, a green T-shirt with lacy sleeves and just one sock. "Sorry," she said as she looped her hair into a ponytail. "Today was my Wednesday off, which you would think means I'd be ready early, except I lost track of time while I was writing, and well… Give me a sec. I need to shut down the computer and get some shoes on."

"And your other sock," he said, following her inside. The living room was filled with books and pictures of her family.

She disappeared around a corner, and when she returned, she had matching socks on and a pair of sneakers in her hand. "I see you found my collection."

He was studying the Snoopy knickknacks on a shelf above her TV.

"Snoopy is my dad's favorite," she said. "Mom used to get him Snoopy greeting cards and Christmas ornaments every year. Guess I picked it up from him."

His gaze landed on a figurine of Snoopy typing,

hard at work on a story. "I can see why." He turned to face her. "Since you looked me up on the internet, it only seemed fair for me to do the same. Your stories are great."

She froze in the act of tying a shoe. "You read one?"

"Three, actually. Last night." He frowned. "Is that okay?" He never would've mentioned them if he hadn't liked them. "I mean, they were published for people to read. Right?"

"Yes, of course. I want people to read them, but at the same time, they're…part of me. Having people read them means being exposed—naked, in a way."

His gaze dropped over her body. "For the record, I'm pro-naked."

Her cheeks reddened, but she returned his smile as she stood. "You really liked them?"

"They were fantastic and eerie as hell." He took a step forward and tapped her forehead lightly. "There's some surprisingly dark stuff behind those gorgeous eyes of yours."

Her smile grew, and she wrapped one arm around him. "Hell of a compliment."

"That I think you have beautiful eyes?"

"That you think I'm dark and twisted. Just what every budding suspense author wants."

Cupping her face, he leaned closer. "Well, if there's anything else you want… I aim to please." Their kiss was thorough and languid, the kind of leisurely exploration they hadn't had time for until now because there'd been other people around.

But we're alone now. That realization, along with

Hadley's soft purr of pleasure, shot heat to his groin. He kissed a trail down the side of her neck, and she tipped back her head, giving him access to the hollow of her throat.

He swallowed. "We should probably get going, huh?" It was their first date. Probably too soon to toss her onto the nearest horizontal surface.

She looked dazed as she met his eyes. "Yeah. Probably." She drew a ragged breath. "Grayson, I…"

In her face, he saw the same conflicting impulses he felt, and he kissed her gently. "Me, too."

They moved toward the door faster than was strictly necessary, as if they needed to leave before they changed their minds, and neither of them said much as he started up his truck. The silence in the cab was charged, and he turned on the air-conditioning even though the evening was cool.

"Music?" he asked. He turned the radio knob, and a heavy beat filled the space between them as the singer rhapsodized about the things she wanted her lover to do to her. Wincing, Grayson turned off the radio. "Maybe not."

Next to him, Hadley choked back a laugh.

Neutral topic, neutral topic. Bowling shoes weren't sexy. As he drove toward the bowling alley, he asked her about the playfully boasting text she'd sent earlier. "You seem pretty confident that you'll win. How'd you get so good at bowling?"

"My dad. He used to be in the league, and he'd take me with him to practice after school."

"Sounds like you and your dad are pretty close."

"Very. He's the one who taught me to pitch. He cheered his head off for me at all my softball games. Mom loved me, of course, but it's like she never knew what to do with me. She and Leanne had a lot in common. When Leanne fell for the wrong guy and followed him out of state, Mom was brokenhearted. I felt like nothing I did made up for Leanne's absence. Until Mom's stroke. She and I spent days on end together, and, for the first time, we really started to understand each other. Not that I'm happy she had the stroke," she added hastily.

"Of course not. You're just finding the good in something horrible that happened. I admire that about you. Until recently, I wasn't much of a silver-lining guy. When bad things happened, I got angry and held a grudge."

"That must get emotionally exhausting. You can't prevent bad things from happening," she said softly. "So you might as well look for the good."

"I'm working on it." He didn't want the boys going through life ticked off, and, besides, Hadley was right. Being mad all the time took a lot out of a person.

His mind went to Violet's confession, about knowing where his mother was. After Vi gave him his mom's phone number, he'd stuck it at the bottom of a duffel bag in his closet. He didn't want to waste time thinking about Rachel; evidence suggested she certainly hadn't thought much about him. But was pushing aside all thoughts of her an indication that he didn't care, or just a sign that, deep down, he was still angry?

"Can I ask your opinion?" he asked.

"In Cupid's Bow, you don't even have to ask. People just give them freely."

He attempted a smile, but it didn't take.

"What's up?"

"You know my mom left when I was in first grade? Just walked out. Left a note telling my father goodbye and saying to give me a hug on her behalf. Yeah," he said bitterly, "because a hug is definitely enough to cancel out two decades of wondering why she didn't love you and if you'll ever see her again."

Hadley made a small sound but didn't interrupt.

"When her father died, I thought maybe she'd come home for his funeral, but we didn't hear a word from her. Then *my* dad died. But still nothing."

"Ever look for her on the internet?" she asked.

"Of course. I got a few million unhelpful hits. A competitive eater in Chicago, British tabloid coverage of a model from Edinburgh. And an obituary, which scared the hell out of me until I realized it was for a ninety-four-year-old woman. After that, I couldn't quite bring myself to try again for a long time. Miranda—the twins' mom—once suggested I hire a PI so I started saving up money to do that. Then I thought, *why*? Why spend my hard-earned cash to track down a woman who wanted nothing to do with me? So I decided to just stop thinking about her." He stared out the windshield, wondering how he would have reacted if Vi had given him the choice when he was a teenager, if he would have gone with Rachel.

"But you're thinking about her now. Because you're back in Cupid's Bow?"

"Because Violet told me she's been keeping a secret. When we were in high school, my mom showed up, a married woman who wanted me to come live with her and her husband."

Hadley gasped. "And Violet didn't tell you?"

"Not until recently. I don't know that I fault her for it. Who's to say my mom really wanted me? As soon as Violet said no, she left without putting up much protest or trying to see me. What if I'd gone with her and she and her husband eventually had a kid of their own? Would she send me back because I was extraneous?"

"She'd be crazy to give up free built-in babysitting."

He snorted; an offbeat sense of humor was more soothing than pity. "Anyway, when Vi told me the truth, she gave me my mother's phone number. Or at least, the last known number we have. If you were me...would you call? I haven't spoken to the woman in twenty-one years."

"If I were you? That's a tough one. I've been told I have unhealthy levels of curiosity. Whether or not calling is what's best for you, though..."

He turned left, the blue neon letters of the bowling alley ahead. "This is a weird first-date conversation, isn't it? We're supposed to be talking about our favorite movies or something."

"My favorite movie is based on one of my favorite books, and when I get carried away comparing what I love about each of them, people tend to get glassy-eyed and fake incoming phone calls to escape. But I'm flattered you trusted me with something so personal." She gave him a rueful smile. "I just wish I had a better answer to give you because, honestly, I don't know what you should do. She hurt you badly. Why give her the chance to do it again?"

He parked the truck and unfastened his seat belt.

"On the other hand," Hadley said as she opened her door, "life is uncertain. Chances at closure don't last forever. If you don't at least try, how much will you regret it down the road?"

Chapter Eleven

"The food here is better than I expected," Grayson said.

"Too bad," Hadley said, raising her voice to be heard over the erratic rhythm of bowling balls roaring down the lane into the pins.

He frowned. "Why is it a shame that I like the food?"

"Because if you didn't, I could finish your fries for you." She grinned, completely without shame when it came to potatoes. She'd once arm-wrestled her sister over the last of their mom's sinfully cheesy au gratin.

Grayson laughed. "Maybe we should get another order to split."

"We can after we bowl." She raised an eyebrow. "I'm always hungry after kicking ass."

"Big talk. Care to make a wager on—"

"Gambling, Mr. Cox? Tut, tut." Sixteen-year-old Mona Flores paused by their table, holding hands with a boy about an inch shorter than her and who had a pierced eyebrow. "What kind of role model does that while impressionable kids such as myself are around?"

Grayson turned his head, looking surprised but not displeased to see her. "Mona! What are you doing here?"

The girl turned pointedly toward the bowling lanes, then back to him. "Playing racquetball," she replied, deadpan.

He snorted. "I meant, how are you out and about? Last I saw you, there was complaining about your 'ridiculous parents' grounding you for the rest of your natural life."

"Guess this must be my unnatural life then. Hi, Miss Lanier. Thanks for that book you recommended about glass sculpture. The pictures are sick. One day I'll get out of this town and actually see some of those museum exhibits."

"In the meantime, go to your classes," Grayson said. "*All* of them."

"I am." She lifted her chin. "I even got an A minus on my math quiz today, hence the parental units letting me go out to celebrate."

"Nice job." Grayson high-fived her, then turned a flinty glare to her date. "It's a school night. Have her home early."

The boy choked out a startled "yessir" as Mona laughed and dragged him away.

Watching them go, Grayson suddenly paled. "Dear Lord. I really *am* becoming a dad."

Hadley shook her head in mock-pity, charmed but not above heckling him. "We'd better go ahead and bowl before you start yelling at kids to get off your lawn."

They paid their bill for dinner, then headed for the counter, where they rented shoes and signed up for a lane. On weekends, there was usually a significant wait unless you called ahead and reserved one, but tonight, the crowd was moderate, evenly split between the lanes, the diner and the arcade. She was giving the attendant her shoe size when a too familiar voice behind her said, “Hey, puddin’.”

It was her father’s pet name for her. *You have* got *to be kidding me.* She spun around slowly, as if he would vaporize into thin air given enough time. But there he was, grinning, with his arm around her mother’s waist.

“Mom, Dad.” She managed a somewhat strangled introduction. “Grayson, these are my parents. Paul and Wanda Lanier.”

“A pleasure to meet you. Grayson Cox.” He politely shook hands with both of them.

“What are you two doing here?” Hadley tried to make it sound like a cheerful, isn’t-this-a-fun-coincidence question, rather than the blatant accusation it was.

“We were at the church potluck,” Wanda said, “and got to talking to Gayle and Harvey about how much fun it was when we used to go bowling. Then on the way home, your dad said maybe we should pop in for a few frames.”

Uh-huh. That certainly was one possibility. Another was that Hadley had been spotted on her date sometime during the last hour and a dutiful citizen had reported in to her parents. *Maybe we should have just stayed at my place.* Except, based on the heated kisses they'd shared, their physical relationship would have escalated pretty quickly. Hadley wanted Grayson, but she wasn't one for casual sex.

Then again, judging by the wicked intensity of the man's mouth, *casual* wouldn't be the right word to describe it.

Her face heated, and she suddenly realized her mother was staring at her. Damn blushing. It was why she always got busted and Leanne had gotten away with things when they were little.

"Mind if we share a lane?" her dad asked Grayson.

"Not at all. The more, the merrier," her date said gamely.

As the two men walked toward the racks to choose bowling balls, she overheard her father ask, "So what is it you do for a living, Grayson?"

Just what every couple wanted for their first date—burgers, bowling and interrogation.

"Mom..."

Wanda smiled beatifically. "Yes, dear?"

Hadley mentally searched her vocabulary, censoring the words too inappropriate for using with parents. "I..."

"I'm so glad we ran in to you and your gentleman friend. We've heard so much about him from your sister and Miss Alma and Anne Ross. Why, we were starting to feel left out."

It wasn't quite a guilt trip. More like a guilt casual outing. "Mom, we've only been out a couple of times. You know that if it turns in to something, I would have brought him to meet you and Daddy."

"Well, now you don't have to. It's serendipity."

Once they had all the necessary equipment, her dad bought them a pitcher of soda while Hadley entered their names into the system. She was rattled enough by her parents' appearance that her first attempt was a gutter ball, but she knocked down all ten pins on her next go.

"That's my girl," Paul cheered. To Grayson he said, "I knew she was special even when she was a baby, that she would do great things."

A shadow crossed Gray's face, and Hadley would bet all the overdue fines she'd collected this year that he was thinking about her arm and her lost scholarship. But he rallied. "You're right, sir. She is special."

She beamed at the sincerity in his tone. Maybe the evening wasn't a complete fiasco. Still, the more childhood stories her proud father shared, the more she winced inwardly. Not because the anecdotes embarrassed her, but because of Grayson's past. Was it difficult for him to be around doting parents when his own family life had been such a train wreck?

As they finished up their first game, she quickly shut down the idea of a second. "I'm really tired. Grayson, would you mind taking me home?"

"Or we can," Wanda said. "And your father could take a look at that kitchen light that's been giving you trouble."

"Another time," Hadley said firmly. "Night, guys." She gave each of her parents a kiss on the cheek. On the way out to the truck, she muttered, "If those two follow us to my place, neither of them are getting Christmas gifts ever again."

Grayson laughed. "I like them."

That warmed her heart, given how close-knit her family was. "Thank you. But next date? Just you and me. No family members."

He gave her a sheepish smile. "Is this a bad time to mention I promised the boys I'd invite you to have dinner with us Saturday?"

ALL THE HORSES were in their stalls and Grayson was putting away the last of the equipment when Jarrett entered the barn.

Grayson grinned. "Hey, boss. Almost wrapped up here. Come to check my work?"

"Nope, just wanted to say thanks. With Mom and Dad deciding to spend the weekend in Austin after his cardiology appointment yesterday and Sierra and I meeting with the reverend this afternoon, I would have had to cancel at least four lessons if you hadn't been here."

"I enjoyed it," Grayson said. More than he'd expected, actually. "I've never taught before. The kids were fun." Sam and Tyler were giving him a new perspective on children. But despite liking his work, he'd been looking forward to quitting time. He had a date to prepare for.

Coincidentally, so did Violet. When he'd told her about inviting Hadley over, saying he hoped it wouldn't inconvenience Vi, his aunt said she wouldn't even be home Saturday night. She'd shyly admitted that she was going to dinner and a movie. With Jim. Grayson couldn't be happier for them.

"Want to stop by the house for a cold drink before you head out?" Jarrett offered.

"Raincheck for another time? I promised a pretty librarian a home-cooked meal tonight."

"You cook?" Jarrett looked impressed. He'd told Grayson before that he had exactly one culinary skill—grilling steak.

"Vi attempted to teach me, but I was a horrible student. I didn't bother measuring right or I'd get impatient. So, before I moved out on my own, she taught me one surefire meal—pot roast in a slow cooker. There are fewer than ten ingredients, and it's impossible to screw up. I just hope it doesn't raise Hadley's expectations, because the rest of my repertoire is pretty hit-or-miss."

Jarrett chuckled. "From the way she looks at you, I don't think you're gonna scare her off with rubbery pasta or a burned entrée."

"Well, I might scare her off if I show up smelling like sweat and horses. I'd better get home so I have plenty of time to shower. See you tomorrow."

Cupid's Bow didn't have some of the amenities of bigger cities, but that meant no city traffic, either. He made it to the farmhouse in good time, and the delicious aroma of roast hit him as soon as he opened the door.

"The boys have been asking every five minutes if it's time to eat yet," Violet said as he entered.

"I don't blame them." He straightened from taking

off his boots and got his first real look at her. "Excuse me, miss, have you seen my aunt anywhere? About yay tall, lives in T-shirts and yoga pants?"

"Ha, ha." But there was a touch of nervousness in her expression. "When you work at home, there's no reason to wear dresses every day. Or makeup."

"Well, you look great." But it wasn't the clothes or cosmetics. It was the sparkle in her eyes and happy glow about her that made the real difference. "Have fun tonight. When's he picking you up?"

She checked the slim gold watch around her wrist. "Fifteen minutes. As long as you hurry, I can watch the boys while you shower."

"Thanks. And don't let them near the pot roast!"

By the time Hadley rang the doorbell half an hour later, he was cleaned up, Violet had left and the hungry five-year-olds had been placated with cheese-and-cracker appetizers.

Hadley inhaled appreciatively. "Dinner smells incredible."

"I cooked it myself," he boasted. "Well, actually the Crock-Pot cooked it, but I threw in the ingredients and turned on the pot, so I'm taking credit. Now, before I pull the plates down, should I be setting the table for your parents, too, or will it just be us?"

She laugh-groaned. "If they show up, I'm talking to Sheriff Trent about some kind of restraining order."

From somewhere within the house there was a loud crash.

He clapped a palm to his head. "We'd better see what the twins have knocked over now."

They found the boys in the back hall, trying to shove flowers into a broken vase.

Sam's expression was stricken. "We were just tryin' to get one to give to Hadley."

Grayson gave his date a sheepish smile. "I've been outclassed by five-year-olds. *I* should've thought of flowers. I'm not much of a romantic."

"You have your moments," she reassured him. "As for you two..." She kneeled to fold the twins into a hug. "It's the thought that counts, so thank you for my flowers."

Watching her cuddle the boys close made Grayson's lungs feel tight. One of his biggest regrets at that moment was that Blaine and Miranda would never meet Hadley. *You guys would love her.*

Once the broken vase was cleaned up, they moved on to dinner. The boys were so excited by their guest that Grayson barely got a word in edgewise. But he didn't mind. It was deeply satisfying to watch three of his favorite people interact. It was also wildly entertaining. He gave up eating halfway through the meal because the twins' kindergarten tales made him laugh so hard, he was afraid he might choke.

"We finished all our food." Tyler wrinkled his nose. "Even the salad. Can we play a game now?"

Violet had taken the boys to a toy store downtown and let them pick out a few inexpensive board games.

"*One* game," Grayson intoned. "After that, story time and bed."

Somehow, one game turned into three, with Hadley laughing at Grayson's frustration that he couldn't build a bug. Everyone else had a brightly colored plastic bug with pieces they'd assembled by rolling dice on their turns—bodies with legs, heads that had eyes and antennas. Sam only needed to roll the number six for a mouth to win the game. All Grayson had was a collection of feet.

"Maybe you should stick to bowling," Hadley said. "This doesn't seem to be your game."

"Tyler, hand me the rules," Grayson said. "I think we forgot to read the part where the person with the most feet gets bonus points."

Hadley shook her head. "Boys, don't you think there should be a penalty for attempted cheating? When I was growing up, the punishment was…being tickled!"

They all three pounced on Grayson, who fought back. The living room echoed with laughter and shrieking. Grayson couldn't tell if the breathless antics were tiring the boys out or just winding them up. But, finally, he and Hadley convinced them that they had to get ready for bed in order to hear a story.

While she read to them, Grayson cleaned up the kitchen, then returned to the dimly lit bedroom, noting how beautiful she was bathed in lamplight. And the boys, snuggled on either side of her, looked cherubic. Last weekend had thrown Grayson some curveballs, finding out about Rachel and about Hadley's arm, but now he felt…dangerously happy. It wasn't an emotion he was comfortable with. Too many times in his life, joy had been overturned by tragedy. His self-preservation instincts fought against contentment.

"Okay," he said gruffly, "that's enough for tonight. Time to go to sleep."

Hadley slid out from between the boys, but Sam tugged on her sleeve.

"Can you help tuck us in?" Sam asked.

She kissed his forehead. "It would be an honor."

"What's an honor?" Tyler asked around a yawn.

"We'll save that for the next time I come over," Hadley said. "I'll bring a book about an honorable knight who lives in an enchanted castle."

The four of them shared hugs and night-night prayers, and Grayson tried to squelch the voice inside that asked if it was wise to let the boys get so attached to her. *How can I stop them when I can't even stop myself?*

Chapter Twelve

Hadley scanned the book with a grin. "Someone's planning to do an impressive amount of reading. I approve."

On the other side of the counter, Sandra Feller shrugged. "Might as well do something with all my sleepless hours."

"Having trouble with insomnia?" Hadley asked. She'd heard it could be a long-term effect of chemo. Hopefully, now that Sandra was all done with her treatments, the side effects would fade.

"It's the darnedest thing. I nod off just fine, but I can't *stay* asleep. The cats think I'm nuts, prowling the house at odd hours. They're like 'hey, that's our job.'"

Hadley laughed. "Well..." Movement in her peripheral vision distracted her, and she turned to see Grayson striding into the library. He wore jeans and a dark T-shirt, and his hair was damp, as if he'd recently showered.

He met her gaze, and a smile broke across his handsome face. Warmth spread through her as if she had liquid sunshine in her veins. They'd been spending enough time together that one might think she'd stop reacting so strongly whenever she saw him. But just the opposite was true.

She suddenly became aware that Mrs. Feller was watching her with raised eyebrows. "Mrs. Feller, do you know my friend Grayson Cox? We're on the Watermelon Festival committee together."

Mrs. Feller turned to study him, her green eyes shrewd. "I don't believe we've met. Officially."

"Uh, no, ma'am." He shook her hand, darting a nervous glance toward Hadley. "Grayson Cox."

"Violet Duncan's nephew, correct?" At his nod, she added, "And quite a firebrand in your youth, as I recall."

Hadley was a bit surprised by this description since Grayson had gotten away with his antics. Did many people know he'd been a troublemaker? Then again, aside from some fuzzy moments during her illness, Mrs. Feller was sharp as a tack. Hard to get much past her.

"Yes, I was," Grayson admitted.

Hadley nodded to the tote bag on Mrs. Feller's shoulder. "Want me to put your books in the bag for you?"

Mrs. Feller nodded, but before handing over the bag, she shuffled through the stack of books until she found the only nonfiction title she'd checked out. It was about the care of roses. "Do you know, Hadley, some Good Samaritan planted roses in front of my house?"

Hadley kept her gaze on the books. "Well, that's…

Are you happy about them? They're not causing you too much work, are they?"

Mrs. Feller laughed. "A little work is good for a body. And you know how I love my flowers. I hope whoever did the kind act knows it was appreciated," she said as Hadley returned the now full bag.

"They're due back in a week, but you're welcome to renew them online," Hadley said.

"See you next week." Mrs. Feller turned and gave Grayson a small smile. "Nice to meet you, son. Officially."

As she exited the building, Grayson cleared his throat. "Does everyone else feel like she can see into their soul, or is that just my guilty conscience?"

She would have poked fun at someone else having the overactive imagination for once except that sometimes talking to Mrs. Feller did feel like that. "She is frighteningly observant."

"You didn't warn me you were sending me to plant flowers for a psychic."

"And *you* didn't warn me you'd be stopping by." She hoped he hadn't been planning to surprise her with lunch, which would be an incredibly thoughtful schedule conflict. "I'm leaving in five minutes." Bunny was coming in to relieve her, then Hadley was meeting Becca.

"Me, too, actually. I'm headed to the elementary school, today's mystery reader for Ms. Baker's kindergarten class. Help me pick out a book?"

She gave him two stories and a few stolen kisses behind the reference books before sending him on his way. As she watched him leave, she sighed happily. A sexy cowboy who made time to read to small children? *I am a lucky, lucky woman.*

AT THE ELEMENTARY SCHOOL, Grayson remembered this time to ring the buzzer and went into the main office to get a visitor's pass.

The woman behind the desk pursed her lips and stared hard, as if trying to place him. "Oh! You're Hadley Lanier's boyfriend, aren't you?"

"I..." They hadn't labeled their relationship, and, frankly, he preferred it that way. If he thought too hard about what was happening, panic came rushing in.

A little girl opened the door behind him, saying she needed to see the nurse, and he slipped out without addressing the woman's question.

He waited outside Ms. Baker's classroom for the teacher to announce him. All the kids were sitting in a circle on the carpet with their eyes closed; he wondered how she kept that many five-year-olds from peeking. He settled into the rocking chair at the front, and she told the children to open their eyes.

Tyler gaped in surprise, but Sam's face radiated excitement to see him.

"Everyone say hi to Mr. Cox, who—"

A little girl in pigtails leaned forward to ask Tyler and Sam, "Is that your daddy?"

The twins shared a long look and answered in unison. "Yes."

Grayson opened the first book, his heart full.

Again, he had that niggling sense that he was in

over his head. When was the last time in his life he'd had so many people he cared this deeply about? He thought of the romantic movie he'd watched with Hadley Saturday night and tried to cling to her optimistic belief in happy endings.

Of course, for all her love of the hero winning the day, she also wrote suspenseful stories full of death and darkness. Life was both, the dark and the light, and you rarely got to choose which came for you.

A COMPETITIVE PERSON, Hadley didn't know whether she was annoyed she'd lost at Scrabble or turned on that Grayson was such a worthy adversary.

Turned on, she decided. Of course, she'd pretty much felt that way ever since he arrived at her place for dinner. The last two hours of conversation and Scrabble by candlelight had only heightened her desire for him.

Last two hours? Try the last two weeks. Every time she saw him, she fell for him a little more. Part of her wondered if that was wise, but he kept making dates with her. She knew she wasn't alone in her growing feelings. And, tonight, she didn't want to be alone in her bed. The privacy at Grayson's place was limited, but they were at her house tonight. She'd wondered if, given the opportunity, he might try to seduce her. If not, was she brave enough to take the initiative?

Maybe she hadn't been before Grayson, but the way he looked at her, the way he kissed her, was emboldening. Leanne had told her not too long ago that

Hadley needed to work on her confidence. *Mission accomplished.*

She carried the board game to the closet. As she shut the door, Grayson joined her, moving with that rugged grace she so enjoyed watching.

"I think the winner should get a kiss," he told her.

She grinned. "That works out pretty well for the loser, too."

He backed her against the wall, his mouth claiming hers. She was glad for the support behind her when he grazed his teeth over the sensitive slope of her neck and her knees went weak.

He raised his head to meet her eyes, but his hand continued to swirl distracting patterns across her collarbone and beneath the straps of her brightly colored sundress. "All of my blood is rushing south," he told her, "so while I can still think straight, I just want to say…thank you. For dinner tonight and for everything you've done for me since I got here."

"If you'd like to do something for *me*…" She slid her hand down to the waistband of his pants and crooked a finger through his belt loop. "Stay the night?"

He groaned. "I need to get home before the boys wake up for school, but that still gives us hours."

"Hours, hmm? We can do a lot in that time." She led him to her room, where she picked up the remote that controlled a trio of electric candles. She couldn't wait to get him out of his shirt, to see the flicker of candlelight across the hard muscles of his chest.

He cupped her face, not kissing her yet, just studying her expression.

"In case you're wondering what I'm thinking," she said, "it's how much I want to get you naked."

He gave a rusty laugh. "Feeling's mutual."

Between kisses and intimate touches, they undressed each other with more enthusiasm than finesse, and she couldn't stifle a moan of appreciation at the sight of his naked form. Then she was moaning because his hands were at her breasts, caressing and teasing. Pleasure sang through the most feminine parts of her. They tumbled onto the bed, rolling across the mattress toward the condoms in her nightstand.

"You're sure this isn't moving too fast for you?" he asked, double-checking before he opened the foil packet she'd handed him.

She arched her back, circling her hips against him in a way that made his breath hiss. "I want to feel you moving fast. And deep. And—"

He covered her mouth with a hungry kiss, then he was inside her, wringing more desire from her than she would have imagined possible. And she had one hell of an imagination.

His face was starkly beautiful in the moonlight as he held himself above her. "You feel amazing."

She clenched around him as he found the perfect angle, and words were lost in gasps and ecstatic cries. When the first tremors of her climax began, he lowered his head to her breast, sucking until her body bowed in a devastating orgasm.

There was definitely nothing "casual" about sex with Grayson. He'd just ruined her for all other men, and she was too breathlessly happy to care.

HADLEY CAME AWAKE INSTANTLY, not because the soft rustling in the dark was much of a disturbance, but because she was so used to sleeping alone. The sound of anyone else's movements was foreign. "Grayson?"

He smiled at her from where he stood at the foot of the bed. "I was just getting dressed and debating whether to wake you or leave a note. I hate to leave, but, unfortunately, the boys are early risers. The last thing we want is them telling their kindergarten class about my sleepover with Miss Hadley."

She smiled drowsily. "Call me later?"

He came around the side of the bed to kiss her goodbye. "Of course. But since you're awake now, you should be the first to know. After all, you're the one who inspired me."

Sleepiness gave way to curiosity. "To do what?"

"I've made a decision. You were telling those stories about your family, your parents, last night and I… I'm going to use that phone number Vi gave me."

She sat up straight. "You're going to call your mom?"

"I am. I don't honestly know if I can ever forgive her. But I owe it to myself to try."

AS HE ENTERED San Antonio's city limits, Grayson fumbled through the armrest console for antacids. Nausea and doubt had been his road-trip companions for the past three hours. Had he made a mistake by turning down Vi's offer to come with him?

No, someone had to stay with the boys. Hadley had to work on weekday afternoons and asking her to do something as personal as keeping his godsons overnight and getting them ready for school tomorrow felt like taking their relationship to another level. He wasn't ready for that. He was still processing how incredible sex with her had been. How intimate.

A sports car zipped into the lane in front of him without using a blinker, and Grayson made himself focus on the road. He could wallow in self-doubt once he'd reached the hotel. The plan was for him to text Rachel after he'd checked in, and then they could meet for dinner. He would drive back tomorrow, but what time he left would depend on how tonight went. Would she want to introduce him to her husband? Would they have breakfast together before he returned to Cupid's Bow?

Of course, both of those possibilities assumed that she even showed up tonight. The virtual stranger who'd given birth to him didn't have a track record of being dependable.

It was difficult to tell from their short, stilted phone conversation if she was looking forward to seeing him. He'd called from the house. Seeing the number, she'd answered expecting her sister.

"Violet? Is everything okay?" she'd asked.

"Actually, this is Grayson," he'd responded. "And we're fine. Vi decided it was time to tell me where to find you. And I decided it was time you and I talked. Preferably, in person."

"All right."

Only the two words, uttered without inflection. She hadn't volunteered to come to Cupid's Bow, which was just as well. He couldn't begin to know how to explain her to the twins. So, he'd said he would drive to San Antonio and asked her what the best night to meet was.

Now, here he was, checking in to a motel just off the freeway on a Tuesday afternoon. He didn't even know if she was still married to the same guy or if she'd eventually had other children. What if she didn't show up to dinner alone? *Guess I'll know soon enough.*

He texted her that he'd arrived safe and sound, and she directed him to a Tex-Mex restaurant on the famed San Antonio River Walk. The tourist destination struck him as a little surreal. He hadn't driven all this way to take in the sights; he'd come to… What? Find closure? Make a fresh start? Look her in the eye and ask once and for all, "why the hell did you do it?"

When he arrived at the cantina, the hostess told him his party had already arrived and showed him to a booth in the back. Grayson's first sight of the well-dressed strawberry blonde made blood pound in his ears. She didn't look as different as he'd expected. She was aging gracefully. Of course, she'd only been twenty when she'd had him.

She stood when he reached the table, but didn't make a move toward him. A hug seemed awkward to the point of physical pain, and a handshake would just be weird. What was the protocol here? A fist bump?

"Grayson. You look good," she said shakily. "You look like Bryant. He was a handsome devil, too."

Not toward the end, he wasn't. He'd been constantly disheveled with bloodshot eyes, a bloated face and a red nose. "Thank you." He sat on the bench opposite her, and the waitress asked if she could start them off with cocktails.

"Vodka martini, extra olives," Rachel ordered.

"Just ice water for me." Although, if there was ever a time he'd been tempted to imbibe, it was now.

When they were left alone, she reached up as if to tuck her hair behind her ear, apparently forgetting she'd smoothed it all into a twist. Nervous habit?

"Times like this, I wish I still smoked," she admitted.

"I don't remember you smoking."

"That came later."

He knew so little about her. "Do you have kids?" he blurted. When she blinked at the abrupt question, he apologized. "Sorry. It occurred to me on the drive today that I might have brothers or sisters I've never met."

"No," she said softly. "No children besides you. Probably a good thing, huh? Not exactly Mother of the Year over here."

That would depend on the year. For the first six years of his life, he'd felt loved and safe, which made everything that came after an even bigger betrayal.

"What about you?" she asked. "Wife? Kids?"

"I'm not married, but I have custody of two boys. They aren't mine biologically, but I was close to their parents. They've passed away," he explained, his voice so low it was barely audible.

Their drinks arrived, and Rachel grabbed hers like a lifeline, wrapping perfectly manicured fingers around the stem before gulping down chilled vodka.

The waitress's eyes widened fractionally, but she didn't comment except to ask if they were ready to order.

"Shrimp soft tacos," Rachel said.

"And a combo number six for me." Grayson handed over his menu wistfully. Studying the choices had given him something to do besides make eye contact with the woman across from him.

Silence descended across the booth like a thick fog.

After two more slugs of her martini, she offered, "I was sorry to hear about your father. I had no idea he'd died until I ran in to an old acquaintance."

"And that's when you visited Violet?"

She averted her gaze. "Shortly after that, yes."

"Why *did* you go see Vi?"

"Many reasons. To check on you, to mourn the loss of my own dad, to ask her about you living with me and Cooper. My husband. We're coming up on our fifteenth anniversary."

"But Vi said no, so you just took off again? It was Cupid's Bow. If you'd wanted to see me, it would have been easy."

"My sister knows you better than I do. When she told me what she thought was best, I respected her wishes." She said it so matter-of-factly, as if walking away from him a second time had been simple. Hell, maybe it had been. She'd managed it easily enough the first time.

She's not even sorry. Could he forgive someone who didn't show an ounce of remorse over hurting the people closest to her?

"This was a mistake," he said stiffly. He pulled

some tens from his wallet and tossed them on the table to cover his meal. "I'm sorry I wasted your time." Maybe she could get his dinner to-go and take it home to Cooper.

In one fluid motion, he was out of his seat and headed for the door. Behind him, he heard her tell the waitress to cancel their food.

"Grayson, wait!"

He stopped, but not until he'd stepped outside, where the cool evening air was a blessed relief. "I don't think I can do this."

"*You* called *me*."

A mistake, clearly. He didn't bother stating the obvious.

"It's a nice night," she said. "Why don't we walk for a few minutes?"

They did, in silence. Music and chatter spilled out of the restaurants they passed, and he could hear the tour guide on a passing boat tell tourists about the area.

Finally, Rachel asked, "Would you feel better if you just yelled at me? Got it out of your system?"

Somehow, he doubted it would be that easy. "I've only been raising my godsons for a month, and I can't imagine *ever* walking out on them. But you left me without looking back, like it was nothing. How do you live with yourself?"

"You can judge me, but you don't know what it was like. I was nineteen when I met Bryant. I was still trying to decide what I wanted to be when I grew up, when suddenly I was pregnant and had to get married. It happened so fast, I didn't get the chance to think about whether it was what I wanted. I moved straight from my father's house to my husband's. Then one day a girlfriend I hadn't seen in a while called, wanting a bunch of us to go to Vegas for her thirtieth birthday. And I realized thirty was only a few years away. I was almost thirty, and I'd never been anywhere or done anything. All I had to show for my life was a husband I'd felt pressured to marry and a kid I—"

"Didn't want?" he asked roughly.

"Didn't intentionally conceive." It was an awkward save…too little, too late. "In my own way, I did love you, Grayson. But I resented you, too. I'd hoped that, once I was gone, your dad would remarry. Maybe someone closer to his own age, maybe someone who'd always wanted to be a mother."

"The closest thing Dad had to a relationship after you left was his affair with booze."

She flinched. "I had no idea that would happen. Grayson, I know how melodramatic this must sound, but at the time I felt like I was suffocating. Not metaphorically. I literally woke up one morning feeling like I might die if I didn't escape."

That was how he'd felt by the time he graduated. Yet it hadn't been enough to make him sever all family ties.

He stopped, leaning against a pillar beneath a pedestrian bridge. "Thank you." Her explanation hadn't made him feel any better, but at least he finally had one. "When I was a kid, I tortured myself with endless wondering. Had you been kidnapped? Had you joined the CIA? Had you been wooed away from dad by another man you loved more than you loved us? At least now I know."

She sighed. "I know how selfish it is, how much I suck. Why do you think I kept my distance? Violet is awesome. Even when we were kids, she was the responsible one. My little sister used to have to remind me to brush my teeth. So I knew she'd make sure you brushed yours."

It was difficult to argue with that; Violet *was* awesome.

She gave him a once-over that almost qualified as motherly. "You look well, strong and healthy. Are you happy?"

He thought about the events of the past month, the unexpected comfort of coming home and the bittersweet joy of hugging the boys each night, knowing their parents wouldn't get to see them grow up. And Hadley. She was rapidly taking up a space in his heart that alternately thrilled and terrified him. "I don't know."

She nodded. "If you ever find yourself in San Antonio again, feel free to call." The offer seemed more obligatory than encouraging.

"Okay," he said, knowing he wouldn't.

She looked for a second as if she might hug him goodbye, and he stiffened involuntarily. She pressed a cool hand against his cheek, smiled sadly and walked away.

He watched her go through blurred vision. Thoughts rioting, he returned to his hotel room. It was still and lonely. He had his cell phone in hand and considered calling Hadley. God he wanted to hear her voice. But she'd want to know how tonight had gone. Even if she was too tactful to ask, the weight of her unspoken curiosity would crush him. Talking about tonight's aborted encounter would be like picking at a fresh wound when all he wanted was to let it scab over and heal. So instead he turned on the TV, crawled into bed and missed her like crazy.

AS HE PARKED down the street from the feed-supply store, Grayson blinked, almost surprised by his destination. When on his drive back to Cupid's Bow had he made the decision to come here?

He didn't know, but this felt right.

Inside the store, Ned was ringing up a riding blanket and rope lead for a customer. Grayson waited patiently until the woman left. Ned came around the corner to greet him.

"You're back! Might I hope this indicates a change of heart?" the older man asked gently.

Grayson swallowed. "Is that job offer still open?"

The Cox family, his family, had built this store once upon a time. Now Ned was giving him a chance to be part of its legacy. Grayson needed a legacy beyond a father who drank and a selfish mother who just didn't give a damn. And who knew? Maybe one day, the place would be his and the boys could be part of its future, whether they wanted summer jobs during high school or to eventually invest in it themselves.

Ned smiled slyly. "I took the liberty of crunching numbers. Just in case." He gestured toward the small office behind the cash register. "Come, we'll have bad coffee and talk shop."

Grayson laughed. "Best offer I've had all week."

VIOLET MET GRAYSON at the door. No doubt the dogs' ruckus had alerted her that he was here. She enveloped him in a hug that smelled like cinnamon and vanilla.

He inhaled deeply. "You made me cookies."

"On a scale of one to ten, how terrible was it?"

"Eleventy billion."

She squeezed him hard. "I made a *lot* of cookies."

He choked out a laugh, pulling back to look her in the eye. "I know you're too damn young to be a parent to someone my age, much less a grandparent to the boys, but you're the only mom I had in any way that matters and I love you."

Vi burst into tears.

"Oh, hell. Please don't cry."

She wailed something he couldn't make out, but he thought the words *happy tears* were in there somewhere. How long did they have until the boys' school bus dropped them off at the top of the driveway? Hopefully, he would have his aunt calmed down by then.

They went into the kitchen, her sniffling the entire way, the dogs circling in concern. He almost tripped over Shep twice.

There was a tissue box on the far side of the room, but Vi just grabbed a sheet off the paper-towel roll and blew her nose loudly. "Crap, I'm a mess."

"I'm beginning to think we all are."

"I didn't mean to dissolve into tears. My emotions

are running high because I didn't get any sleep. I was so worried about you, kicking myself for letting you go alone, and eventually I texted Jim for moral support. We were on the phone all night." A hint of a smile ghosted her lips.

He grinned. "So that's going well, I take it."

"I'm seeing him again this weekend. Actually, he mentioned a carnival in Turtle. We could take the boys, give you space to mull everything over."

He'd had his fill of mulling in the truck and in the hotel room, but he could use the child-free time to socialize with his friends. Maybe Jarrett and Sierra would like to go out with him and Hadley. Not only did Grayson truly like the rancher and his feisty fiancée, but their presence would also be a helpful buffer, dissuading Hadley from asking about personal topics he wasn't ready to poke at. He should call her, let her know he was back safely.

He left a voice mail for her, mentioning his idea for a double date, then showered off his road-trip grime before the boys got home. They were a little clingier than usual after his absence, but their hugs and silly knock-knock jokes were a balm. During dinner, Sam called him *Dad* several times, as if the word was a newly discovered talisman that could keep away bad things.

I'll do what I can, buddy.

While he was reading them their bedtime story, his cell phone buzzed. The screen flashed with a photo he'd taken of Hadley during the reunion. He hit Decline; she'd understand if he called her back tomorrow.

Sam smiled at her picture. "If you're our new daddy, does that mean Hadley's our new mommy?"

"But I thought Vi is our new mommy," Tyler said.

Grayson's temples throbbed. Mothers were the last thing he wanted to discuss right now. "Vi is your aunt. That's another kind of relative, like a mom. She's family, and she loves you." This might've been an easier concept for them to grasp if Blaine and Miranda hadn't been only children.

"What about Miss Hadley?" Sam persisted.

Crap. Why hadn't he done more to keep a healthy distance between her and the boys? *You knew this was a risk.* Grayson's relationship with her was still new—they'd only slept together once!—and already the twins thought the four of them were a family. Was he setting them up to be hurt the way he'd been when his mother left? Not that Hadley would ever behave so heartlessly, but she had her own path to follow.

Maybe we should slow things down a little.

Except that he was falling for her. And it was damn hard to slow down a free fall.

Chapter Thirteen

A double date with two of her closest friends had sounded fun, but Hadley's mood was melancholy as Grayson pulled his truck into the driveway. She wasn't sure Jarrett had noticed anything amiss while the two men discussed livestock and trucks and the possibility of a fishing trip sometime in May. But Sierra had sent questioning glances across the table, silently asking Hadley what was wrong with her date.

If not for those glances, Hadley might have convinced herself Grayson's distant behavior was a figment of her overactive imagination. He'd been pleasant enough, but she felt like he hadn't looked her directly in the eye all night. On the ride to the restaurant, he'd declared "great song!" and turned the radio volume up to a conversation-discouraging level. It remained that way through the next four songs.

She wasn't stupid. Clearly, he wasn't ready to talk about his visit to San Antonio. So she'd refrained from asking. But after a stilted evening in which he'd barely touched her, she was starting to feel like it was more than just that.

At least he walked her to the front door instead of just dropping her off and peeling out of the driveway. That was something.

As she unlocked the door, he said from behind her, "Sorry it has to be such an early night. Until we finish construction on the church, I'm essentially juggling two jobs—three if you count the riding lessons—and I promised Ned I'd stop by first thing so he can start showing me the ropes. Literally, in the case of a tack store."

She managed a halfhearted smile for the pun. She was actually thrilled for him about the store. Taking the job seemed like a healthy merger of past and future. But she'd been caught off guard to hear the news at the same time as Sierra and Jarrett. Grayson had accepted Mr. Garcia's offer days ago, and this was the first Hadley was learning of it. She'd thought she and Grayson were closer than that, that she mattered more than that.

Or was she simply overreacting because the first man she'd had sex with in a year had bolted out of town almost immediately afterward and hadn't been nearly as affectionate since his return? *Give him time.* Seeing his mother couldn't have been easy. And it wasn't as if he was avoiding Hadley. Their date tonight had been *his* idea.

"Hey," she said, turning to face him, "I'm here for you."

"I know." He looked her in the eye, but only for a moment.

"I realize, however, that my willingness to listen

doesn't necessarily equate your readiness to talk. If you need time to process stuff, that's okay. I don't want to crowd you."

He let out a relieved sigh, taking both of her hands in his. "Really?"

"Loving someone means accepting the ways they're different from you." She hadn't meant to phrase it that way, but it was the truth. She was comfortable owning that. "And I do lov—"

He swept her up in an almost desperate kiss. Because he'd been so moved by her words? Or because he'd wanted to cut off declarations he didn't want to hear?

Out of habit, she kissed him back. But for the first time, she wasn't filled with longing or a rush of desire. When he pulled away from her, she felt as if she might cry.

He squeezed her shoulder. "You're the best, Hadley."

Then why don't you want me?

DON'T CALL HIM, don't call him, don't call him.

Assuring someone you could give him time and space was a meaningless promise if you could barely go twenty-four hours without pestering him. Trying to ignore the cell phone on the kitchen counter behind her, Hadley stuck her head in the fridge and investigated dinner options. She didn't really feel like cooking, but she might as well because she didn't feel like doing anything else, either.

Except for this compulsion to talk to Grayson. *Do*

not be one of those insecure women who drives a man away. She had her own life, her own interests. Maybe she could spend the evening curled up with a good book.

After eating roughly three bites of salad and an entire pint of cookie-dough frozen yogurt, she crawled into bed with a novel by a new author she'd been wanting to try. But after reading the same paragraph four times, she tossed the book onto her nightstand in aggravation. She scooped up her laptop instead. If she was too emotionally distressed to write, there was always Netflix.

When her email pinged, alerting her to an incoming message, she welcomed the distraction. She wouldn't even be mad if it was a money request from a foreign prince. At first, the subject line did seem like junk mail. Congratulations! You've Been Selected...

Her finger hovered over the trash icon, but then she noted the sender's email address, and words started to jump out at her. Like *writer* and *Colorado* and *promising talent.*

I don't believe it. A giddy laugh escaped her as she read, then immediately reread, the entire email. She'd actually been picked to be the writer-in-residence. *Writer* being the key word. Total strangers who dealt in literature for a living thought that she, Hadley Lanier, was a real writer.

She scrambled for her cell phone to call Grayson. Giving a man space to work through a personal issue was one thing, but this was too important not to share. It occurred to her, though, that there was one other call she should make first. After all, it had been her sister who encouraged her to apply in the first place.

"What's up?" Leanne asked. "You caught me on break, but I only have a few more minutes."

"We have to celebrate!" Hadley said. "You are talking to the official writer-in-residence of the Gilded Pages bookstore."

Leanne squealed loudly enough that Hadley moved the phone away from her ear. "Oh, my gosh, I knew you could do it! We have to celebrate this weekend! And go shopping! You need at least one official writerly outfit for the literary events…assuming you're going through with this?"

Hadley frowned. "Why wouldn't I go through with it?"

"I don't know. Because you have a life here? The Watermelon Festival committee, Sierra's wedding stuff." She paused, then added softly, "Grayson."

Hearing his name caused a twinge in her chest. If the man wanted space, he was about to get very good news. "I'm not giving up my dreams for a guy." Not even one as special as Grayson. She would have thought, given Leanne's unhappy past relationships, her sister would understand better than anyone why that was a bad idea.

"Of course not. I just…wasn't sure if you were far enough along in your relationship to handle the stress of long-distance."

Another twinge. Last night, she'd had trouble just handling the stress of a tense dinner date. "If he cares about me as much as I care about him, we'll be able to work this out."

And if he didn't return her feelings? Well, then, maybe it would be best if she wasn't in Cupid's Bow for a while.

"SURPRISE!"

Grayson stared at the sight of Hadley on the front porch, holding a bottle of champagne. "*Surprise* is putting it mildly."

"I have news. I was going to call you, but I really wanted to tell you face-to-face. So I drove over on impulse. I was here before I realized the boys were probably in bed already." Her gaze was apologetic. "I knocked as quietly as I could."

"I'll say. If Shep hadn't whined at the door, I wouldn't have even known you were here."

She peered past him, making him realize he still hadn't let her in. "Is Vi here?"

"No, she's at a movie with Jim."

"Well, I guess that just leaves you and me to drink the sparkling grape juice and celebrate."

He ushered her inside. "What are we celebrating?"

"My being accepted as the writer-in-residence."

"Hadley!" He swept her into a hug that lifted her feet off the ground, spinning her in a quick circle. He was thrilled for her. The last time she'd planned to leave town, Grayson had unwittingly derailed her plans. He sent up a prayer of gratitude that she'd been given this well-deserved second chance.

And selfishly? The timing was perfect. It provided

a natural break to their relationship, and he wouldn't hurt her feelings. That was best for all of them, including the boys, who'd asked tonight when she'd be back for more family games and bedtime stories.

She smiled up at him with shining eyes. "I *told* Leanne you'd be happy for me."

"Of course I am. I'm overjoyed." He led her to the kitchen to see if Aunt Vi had any fancy glasses for the sparkling juice. "Have you told your parents? Your father is going to be so proud."

"Only Leanne. Then I had to come here and share the news with you."

He was touched. After pouring them each a glass, he raised his in salute. "To you."

She clinked her glass against his, radiant in her happiness. This was how she should always look, pleased with her success and excited about her future. He'd hated her tense, pinched expression last night, hated knowing he was the one responsible for it. She was entitled to better than an emotionally stunted man who didn't share her belief in happy endings.

"When do you leave?" he asked.

"Next week." She pressed her hands to her cheeks. "I know I've been dying to hear back from the committee, but now that I have, it feels like it's happening so fast. I'll come back for Sierra's wedding, of course, but I might have to attend her bridal shower virtually. Maybe I could visit for your birthday, too. It's in August, right?"

"Yeah. But Hadley..." The fact that she considered him worth the effort and expense was bittersweet.

"Don't you think it might be better, easier for both of us, if you and I make a clean break?"

"What?" She stared at him, incredulous. "We don't have to break up because of this. I'm going to Colorado, not the moon. And it's only for six months."

"Only? Do you know how long that is to a five-year-old?" He took a deep breath, wanting to find the words that would make her see from his perspective. "The boys are already asking if you're their new mother. They're way too attached."

"*They* are," she said quietly "or you are?"

"Is there an answer here that will make you happy? Yes, I have strong feelings for you—stronger than I'm comfortable with. I told you I don't want a serious relationship. I thought we could keep things between us light. After all, it's only been a few weeks." He brushed a strand of hair away from her face. "Wonderful weeks."

Her eyes shimmered, and she swallowed hard. "Don't you want to give us a chance, to see how wonderful we could be together long-term?"

"No." The idea of that chilled him to the bone. There were so many ways for it to backfire on all of them.

"But Grayson…"

"Dammit. I'm ruining this for you when you should be celebrating. Go to Colorado and be happy."

"You make me happy."

He didn't want that responsibility. "For now. I'm raising cute kids—they make me look good—and I've been on my best behavior for their sake. But I come from selfish, self-destructive people. God only knows the hundred ways I could screw up a relationship. And that doesn't even count all the outside forces that could intervene. I'm not cut out for this, Hadley."

"Maybe you are. I've seen you with the twins. You have a big heart."

A heart he needed to do a better job of protecting. Because right now, there was a miserable ache in his chest. "I know six months might not make up for a four-year college experience, but I accidentally sabotaged your dream last time. Please don't let me ruin it a second time. I don't want you to leave sad about us. Forget about me."

She stared at him disbelievingly before finally shaking her head. "You're an idiot if you think that's how it works. But I'll try my best. Because I'm not going to pine over a man who can't appreciate a great thing when he has it."

So, apparently, I'm a liar. It had been four days since Hadley's vow not to pine over Grayson...and she'd thought about him on every single one of those days. Even now, in the middle of a going-away party in her honor, her gaze continued to stray across the library, hoping to see him come through the doors. Wasn't it possible? That he might miss her as much as she'd been missing him and see the error of his ways?

Maybe not impossible, but certainly improbable.

That's what he'd told her once about happy endings—that they weren't silly, just improbable. So why had she let herself fall for him? Had she really believed that a few weeks together would be enough to change his entire outlook?

"Oh, honey." Kate Trent looked at her with such sympathy that Hadley's eyes burned with tears.

"I'm okay. I'll just miss everyone so much." It was what she'd been telling everyone who caught her on the verge of crying.

Kate knew her too well for that. "And one person in particular?"

She sniffed. "My fault. I stupidly fell for a guy who doesn't want to be in love. He's afraid of it."

"I don't blame him."

Hadley scowled. "Aren't you supposed to be on my side?"

"You know my first husband died. Killed in the line of duty. Do you know how *petrified* I was when I met Cole? To have been that happy once and have it all taken away… I figured, what kind of fool would risk it a second time?"

"But you did." Hadley pointed to the sleeping baby in Kate's arms. "And you're reaping the rewards. How did Cole convince you to stop being afraid?" Because Hadley only had forty-eight hours until she got on the plane, and she was getting desperate.

"He didn't. When I told him I wasn't ready, he respected that. He walked away. It was up to me to conquer my fears."

She sighed. "I have no way of knowing if Grayson will ever conquer his. But I'm definitely walking away…all the way to Colorado."

"I'm so sorry, Hadley. I wish I could fix this for you."

"I wish I could fix it for me, too. But—"

"Miss Hadley!"

Her head jerked up at the sound of Sam's voice. She braced herself just in time for his incoming tackle-hug; his brother was close on his heels. Heart bursting, she scanned the area behind him but only saw Violet.

The other woman shook her head slightly. "We came to say goodbye and good luck. Grayson wanted to come," she said and Hadley wondered if the lie was for her benefit or the boys'. "But he had to work."

Kate greeted the twins. "Hey, you two. Nice to see you again. There's cake. Want a slice?" With Violet's permission, she led them to the refreshment table, giving the two women a moment to talk.

"For what it's worth," Violet said, "he's making a mistake. He was a better person around you, and happier."

"Too happy, I guess. It spooked him." Probably hadn't helped that she'd all but told him she loved him. Still, she didn't regret it. As a kid, he'd had reason to question the love of both his parents. Maybe with enough positive reinforcement, he'd be able to someday accept love. Even if she wasn't the one who benefited from that, she wished it for him.

"Are you okay?" Violet asked kindly.

No. "I will be." Eventually. Meanwhile, she'd seek catharsis in killing off a bunch of fictional characters and hope that her next love story had a happier ending.

Chapter Fourteen

"So, give me all the news from home," Hadley instructed. She wiggled into a comfortable position on the bed, eager to chat with her sister.

Leanne made a dismissive noise. "It's Cupid's Bow. Nothing earth-shattering has happened in the two weeks since you've been gone. Molly and Bunny have the library under control until you get back, one of the Breelan brothers was arrested again. Oh, and Sawyer McCall adopted two kittens without asking Becca first. She's furious, claims she still hasn't forgiven him for bringing home the dog last year."

Hadley laughed at that. "Oh, please. Becca loves that dog. She loves Sawyer, and before you know it, she'll love the kittens, too." *At least someone I know isn't too cowardly to love.* Damn, she'd only made it three minutes into the conversation before thinking of Grayson. She'd been hoping for a record-breaking five minutes this time.

She loved the bookstore where she worked and lived, enjoyed the charm of the surrounding community and was struck by the novelty of getting to know her coworkers. It was fun to spend her days with people who hadn't known her since she was a toddler. Still, when she returned to her loft apartment above the store at night, memories of Grayson haunted her. It was especially bad whenever she talked to anyone from home.

"Enough about the people in Cupid's Bow," Leanne said, clearly bored with the subject. "I want to hear about how it's going there! Did you pick a scene for that reading you're doing next week? Because I have suggestions. And please tell me the cute guy has asked you out."

"I assume you mean Poe?" She'd sent her sister a group shot of Hadley with her new friends. Arthur, the owner, was as full of stories as his shop; he was also sixty. Poe was a doctoral candidate who ran the small coffee shop in the store, and bubbly Jules helped in whichever section needed her the most at any given time. "He's sweet."

"He's cute," Leanne repeated. "Is he single?"

"Apparently." She knew this because Jules and her boyfriend had tried to set up Poe on a blind date last week.

When he'd nixed the idea, Jules had turned a speculative eye toward Hadley. She'd told Hadley that matchmaking was one of her big hobbies, up there with online gaming and playing cello.

"If you're going to meddle in my life," Hadley had said, "I'd rather you introduce me to some addictive video game than to a guy."

Leanne sighed impatiently. "You're not interested in Poe at all, are you?"

"You get how these residencies work, right? I'm supposed to be focused on my writing. I'm not actively looking for romance." She hadn't been actively looking for it in Cupid's Bow, either. She'd just turned the corner of the cereal aisle and stumbled into it.

"Then you'll be sending me the next chapter to proofread soon? You left me on a cruel cliff-hanger last time."

"I'm diabolical like that."

As they hung up the phone, Hadley promised her sister some pages. And she silently promised herself that she'd do a better job of banishing Grayson from her thoughts.

For a few days, she actually succeeded. She went to an outdoor concert with Jules, to a historic hotel rumored to be haunted and wrote two new scenes that didn't completely suck. But on Saturday, as she was ringing up customers, a woman caught her off guard with a purchase from the used-book section. A familiar volume of erotic poetry from the 1930s.

Hadley immediately found herself tangled in a string of memories, from Grayson's expression when he'd seen that same book in the Cupid's Bow library to his playful suggestion of bonus points for erotic words used in Scrabble.

After two attempts, she correctly counted out the woman's change, trying to hold it together as she wished the lady a good day. As soon as the customer exited, she burst into tears.

Jules was at her side instantly. "What happened? You need me to run the cash register while you take five?"

Hadley nodded gratefully, trying to stem the flow of tears.

Jules grimaced. "Poe, a little help over here? He's the one with the talent for making people feel better. I'm useless unless hearing a song on the cello would cheer you up. I wish this was a video game. At least in a game, I could smite your enemies for you."

That almost made Hadley laugh. Except Grayson wasn't her enemy. He was the man she loved, in spite of her best efforts to stop.

"OKAY, TIME FOR some tough love." Vi snapped the dish towel against the counter for effect, and Grayson's head jerked up from the plate of pie she'd offered him after the boys had gone to bed.

"Uh…you have my attention?"

"Good. Because it's like you've been on another planet lately. Or in another state?" she asked shrewdly. "Like, say, Colorado?"

He gritted his teeth. This was not a conversation he wanted to have, but respect kept him from arguing with Vi.

Her tone gentled. "Brokenhearted people are entitled to—"

"I am not brokenhearted!" Hadn't that been the

whole point of letting his relationship with Hadley run its natural course? He'd wanted to guard against devastating pain and loss.

"Fine. People who miss other people are entitled to a little time to wallow. But it's been a month."

"I'm not wallowing, just tired from working two-and-a-half jobs." Now that he'd deposited the money Blaine and Miranda had left him, he could probably afford to let up a little. But he wanted to invest as much of that for the boys' future as possible. Plus, while he knew his aunt would never kick them out, she and Jim were getting more serious by the day. There would come a time when Grayson living under her roof stopped making sense.

"Gray, you've been in a bad mood—bad enough that it's starting to affect the twins."

He flinched. "Have they said something to you?"

"At dinner the other night, when Sam said he missed Hadley? You should've seen your face. He asked me later if you're mad at him, even cried a little bit."

That hit home. "Oh, God. I'll talk to him tomorrow." It was ironic that he'd wanted so much to protect people—himself, Hadley, the boys—and seemed to have failed. The night he'd told her he wanted to make a clean break, she'd looked stricken. Now the boys were miserable because of him?

"I can't tell you who to date or not to date," Violet said, "but I can tell you that I've been where you are. You know I lost my mom when I was little, along with the baby brother I'd been so excited about. Then

Rachel. Walking out on a sibling isn't as unforgivable as abandoning your child, but she left me, too. When I first started dating Jim, I was blown away by how wonderful he was. Happier than I'd been in years. But then I started wondering…how soon before *he* left? Sound familiar?"

He hesitated. This felt like a trap.

"The more I pulled away from Jim, the harder he pressed. We had fault lines in our relationship, and my getting custody of you provided just the earthquake I needed to end it. After fights about what you might be up to and whether I should have told you about Rachel, we broke up. Technically, he made the call, but I let it happen. On some level, I *wanted* it to happen. I told myself you needed me, that you had to be my priority. The truth is, I hid behind you, and I'm sorry. Promise me you aren't doing the same thing with those two sweet boys."

"I'm not hiding. I was setting Hadley free to go after what she wanted!"

"And if what she wants is you? Jim and I are happy now, but I have to deal with knowing that I cheated us out of a decade together. I don't want you to be in my shoes, looking back on a decade with regret, knowing *you* could have been happy. If you'd only been brave enough."

"WELL, BOYS, THIS looks like the place." Grayson glanced at the storefront that he recognized from the website. On either side of him, the twins let out whoops of delight.

The more efficient way to make this trip would have been for him to fly here, alone. But when the boys had heard him discussing plane tickets with Vi, Sam had a panic attack. Given how he'd lost his parents, that was understandable. Eventually, they would work on that phobia, but first, maybe Grayson should conquer his own fears. So he and the boys had plotted a road trip with several stops like a "fossil forest" and a noted planetarium and one theme park. He was becoming so accustomed to being called Dad that he automatically turned now whenever he heard the word in public. He felt closer to the twins than he ever had before, and whatever happened with Hadley, he would always be grateful for this trip.

Still. He hoped like hell that she'd take him back.

He took a deep breath and pushed open the door. "Here goes nothing."

But the boys weren't slowed down by nerves. They barreled into the bookshop, where Sam yelled, "Give us back our librarian!"

Grayson winced. "That's not an appropriate—"

Two store employees approached—one guy, one girl, both in their twenties. They exchanged a look before the girl asked, "Are you by any chance Grayson?"

"Yes, that's Grayson!" Tyler confirmed. "He's our daddy."

The guy with the shaggy hair grinned. "About damn time, man."

HADLEY WAS ENJOYING lunch at her favorite outdoor café and rereading last night's pages when she heard a sudden crash. A waiter's tray clattered to the sidewalk, along with the dishes that had been on it. She glanced over her shoulder in automatic reaction to the sound, but immediately returned to her paragraph.

Until she heard his voice.

"I am so sorry. We'll pay for that. And the food to replace it, of course. The boys are just excited. I asked y'all to stop running."

She bolted out of her chair, whirling around in disbelief. Grayson and the twins, all three wearing matching blue T-shirts, were apologizing to the frazzled waiter. But then Sam spotted her and broke free. He started to run but, thinking better of it, was now speed-walking down the sidewalk toward her.

"Hadley!"

She hugged him tight, the burn of emotion in her throat making it difficult to speak. "What are you doing here?"

"We're on a road trip," he announced. "To get you back."

"Buddy, you're kind of stealing my thunder," Grayson said ruefully.

It was amazing she stayed steady on her feet when she was trembling so badly. "I can't believe it's really you."

Their gazes locked, and from the naked hunger in his eyes, she half expected him to kiss her senseless.

He gave a hard shake of his head. "Is this your table?"

"Um, yes."

"Boys, sit here for a second, okay? Try not to break anything." Then he took Hadley by the hand and led her a few feet away. "You know how the twins are always knocking stuff over?"

"Sure. I guess." No way had he driven all those miles to talk about broken vases or spilled milk. She stared, trying to process the strange lunch hour she was having.

"That's how I feel since you've been gone," he told her. "I'm off balance, crashing through life, making a mess of everything, realizing just how lonely it is to pick up the pieces without your help. I need you, Hadley."

Her breath caught. She was stunned…but cautious. "Are you asking me to come back?"

"Not at all. I'm asking you to let me love you. Whether you're in Cupid's Bow or Colorado or the Congo."

"Seriously?" It wasn't until she tasted salt on her lips that she realized she was crying.

He swiped a tear away with his finger. "Seriously. I missed the whole point of happy endings until recently. They *are* improbable—but only if you aren't willing to work for them. I believe we can do this. If you'll still have me?"

Too overcome to speak, she nodded fervently.

"Thank God." He pulled her against him, and

there was no place she'd rather be. "I love you, Hadley Lanier."

And then he kissed her with such enthusiasm that a few onlookers actually cheered. Two five-year-olds, however, muttered "gross" and made disgusted noises. But when she glanced in their direction, they were both grinning from ear to ear.

Hand in hand, she and Grayson returned to the table.

"So is Hadley coming home?" Sam demanded.

Grayson cast her an apologetic glance. "Sorry, I've tried to explain to him—"

"Not yet," she said gently, "but in a few months. Actually, it will only be a few weeks until I'm home for Sierra's wedding." She grinned at Grayson. "Looks like maybe I have a plus-one now."

"But then you're leaving again?" Sam's lower lip trembled.

"Only temporarily. I'll be gone five months total. That's not so long. You've already made it one whole month without me."

"Yeah, but it stinks," Tyler complained. "And Dad is grouchy *all the time*."

"Hey!" Grayson looked comically indignant. "Who took you to the amusement park, where you said you had the best time ever? You know, if we come visit Hadley once a month until she comes home, we can plan other road trips like this one."

That got the boys' attention.

"And we can talk on the phone and even the computer until I get back," she chimed in. "Maybe you can buy a calendar for your room and put stickers on it for each day until you see me again."

As she paid for her bill and they walked back to the store together, so much joy swelled in her chest she thought her heart would burst with it. Tears blurred her vision.

Grayson squeezed her hand. "Happy?"

"Happier than I ever imagined possible. And you know me—I have a hell of an imagination."

* * * * *

MILLS & BOON

Coming next month

BABY SURPRISE FOR THE
SPANISH BILLIONAIRE
Jessica Gilmore

'Don't you think it's fun to be just a little spontaneous every now and then?' Leo continued, his voice still low, still mesmerising.

No, Anna's mind said firmly, but her mouth didn't get the memo. 'What do you have in mind?'

His mouth curved triumphantly and Anna's breath caught, her mind running with infinite possibilities, her pulse hammering, so loud she could hardly hear him for the rush of blood in her ears.

'Nothing too scary,' he said, his words far more reassuring than his tone. 'What do you say to a well-earned and unscheduled break?'

'We're having a break.'

'A proper break. Let's take out the *La Reina Pirata*—' his voice caressed his boat's name lovingly '—and see where we end up. An afternoon, an evening, out on the waves. What do you say?'

Anna reached for her notebook, as if it were a shield against his siren's song. 'There's too much to do . . .'

'I'm ahead of schedule.'

'We can't just head out with no destination!'

'This coastline is perfectly safe if you know what

you're doing.' He grinned wolfishly. 'I know exactly what I'm doing.'

Anna's stomach lurched even as her whole body tingled. She didn't doubt it. 'I . . .' She couldn't, she shouldn't, she had responsibilities, remember? Lists, more lists, and spreadsheets and budgets, all needing attention.

But Rosa would. Without a backwards glance. She wouldn't even bring a toothbrush.

Remember what happened last time you decided to act like Rosa, her conscience admonished her, but Anna didn't want to remember. Besides, this was different. She wasn't trying to impress anyone; she wasn't ridiculously besotted, she was just an overworked, overtired young woman who wanted to feel, to be, her age for a short while.

'Okay, then,' she said, rising to her feet, enjoying the surprise flaring in Leo di Marquez's far too dark, far too melting eyes. 'Let's go.'